Utriculi

Issue 2 Part 1

2025

Utriculi

Issue 2 Part 1

edited by harry k stammer
contributing editor Mark Young

Cover art by Mark Young
geographies Crystal Brook

Published by Sandy Press (sandy-press.com)

ISSN: 3064-7649
ISBN-13: 979-8-9924582-5-1

Contents

Acknowledgments

Thanks to all who contributed to issue 2 part 1 of Utriculi.

Special thanks to Mark Young for his cover art.
geographies Crystal Brook

Sheila Murphy

Move Over

Move over
overtly.
Halo me be-
yond yon weather-
vane the vein in
your foretaste
bubbling up
through grass-
blades equaling
quality time
for shade I seek
to tweak undreaming
sleep where I nav-
past caring early
to top off
a wanted wanton
vacation from
my constant cosine
mind plural as dandelions
uncertain whether
your certainty fits
this uni- to a tee
its velocity an
ars po- presumed
to suffer when
funding's plucked (un-
lucky for some
like Bingo's B13)
while trying not to
move amid
the unduly plethoral
pinned down apropos
counts heralded
as parsing

distinct from
parch in-
tended to tabulate
in sheaves sleeved
for posthumous
preservation
boning up on
the persistent question
posed in under-
graduate Socratic
recitation *is it*
moral to be
a national near rational
imperial snow globular
wildness trampled
pre-plasticity
unformed
uninformed wearing
our uniforms

My Nest

I can default in a finger snap
to acceptable behavior.

I can be impossible not to live with.
Move closer and decide for yourself.

Hope distances me from introspective
reality, I hear. I fear your logic.

The yogic praxis you belabor contrasts
with my thin skin. I mean guilelessness.

My nest is my unguarded pace
of sitting still with the light closed.

Taxi-Dermabrasion

I am unfinished.
So refinish me.
But don't hang me
on your wall

alongside elk
and falderol revealing
hunting results
and likely accidents.

I am no trophy.
Bear with me
my trope. Believe
the scope in micro-

or macro-hope
called dope. I'm here
dear. Don't want me too
much to display dysplasia.

Cold Brook

Tall hot coffee trespassed on his short attention span.
I'm a good looking guy he said before I thought it
He had a way of not kissing one just because of that.
The way he held a pen the contest between which was best
Say the names you have been taught are authorized to say
Yes charitable donations in my name are welcomed
He was better than you I promise not to want the loss
He first capsized a photograph of me then printed it
What if I'm not beautiful I asked under my breath.
What is here was there more than again as if silhouette
Perfection is a neutral scar in part contagious
Teach children keyboarding on the stiff upright listen then
What supremacy turns back the fold what new premises
Thin Scituate via salt waves crashing against tall rocks

Sheila E. Murphy Appeared in *Verse Daily, Fortnightly Review, Poetry, Hanging Loose,* and others. Most recent book: *Escritoire* (Lavender Ink, 2025). Won the Gertrude Stein Poetry Award for *Letters to Unfinished J.* (Green Integer Press, 2003). Won the Hay(ha)ku Book Prize for *Reporting Live From You Know Where* (Meritage Press, 2018). She lives in Phoenix, Arizona. Her Wikipedia page can be found at: https://en.wikipedia.org/wiki/Sheila_Murphy

Doren Robbins

Poems for the Unborn. John Solt. Shichōsha, Tokyo, August 31, 2020. Poetry.

Audible dreams, Impressions, Observations

Generally, ways of expressing what we don't talk about, or haven't imagined imagining, are not taught; by the sum of their numbers they are infrequently discovered and artistically expressed. In the prose poem "MANIFESTO," from his book, *Poems for the Unborn*, John Solt conveys the alternate uneasy logic of a disrupted coherent sanity within a pathological anti-imaginative social order. Estrangement and self-affirmation explored in the presence of destructive social reality:

MANIFESTO

distortion is what poetry must do. if we don't distort anything, then there is no poetry. so-called reality can be distorted or imagination can be distorted, although some of the reality school might say imagination is already distorted so that would be a redundancy. so-called reality is a distortion of the veneer of imagination. it doesn't matter how the distortion is achieved, as long as there is distortion along the way or at the end. perhaps the ultimate distortion is conning people into thinking that what you think isn't distorted. then you are eligible to become a preacher, a politician or a banker.

if your distorting is merely stress related, it is valid but not art. for your distortion to achieve art, it could use the backing of awards, grants, or kisses on the forehead by fans. big stakes are thrown out for distortion contests, the audience given binoculars with warped lenses.

jimi hendrix was early in generating musical

distortion.

distortion can be achieved in a number of realms.

people are afraid of scientific distortion, called either

human error or mutation.

some might say that out-of-focus on distortion counters the suffering in the reality of the moment and is a political obstacle to liberation of the masses, but it depends what and how people are distorting before their distortion can be interpreted without distortion. small time distorters think that because all is distorted anyway any distortion is equal in proportion or effect to any other. big time distorters know that's all backwards, but lately only the capitalist distorters are being taken seriously by the media distorters which leaves the little guy distorters more distorting, distorted, and distortable than ever.

> i am completely undistorted. (130-132)

By seeing through and taking no part in corporate and institutional representation of the social lie, poetry's "distortion" of the unreal world creates ironic "undistorted" significance. There's no bragging about being "undistorted," the speaker simply isn't passive or fatuous about matter-of-fact inclusion in civilized mass distortion, or subjective exceptionalism. Throughout a lifetime, we have witnessed U.S. presidents touting that the manufacturing and selling of weapons is good for the economy. Therefore, without having to disclose anything factual, peace has tentative or zero financial value, while war profiteering continues to make "distortion" lucrative. Paraphrasing the Chomsky-Herman concept elaborated within *Manufacturing Consent: The Political Economy of the Mass Media,* "distortion" is the result of manufactured or self-deluded public consent. The examples of media manipulated distortion with consumerist allurement appalls the speaker; the counter-examples are the voice representative of millions, possibly billions, of disaffiliated people in the neo-liberal and totalitarian ravagement of contemporary Globalism.

After corporatized government leadership reversed the welfare for the common good inherent in FDR's New Deal, the following poem exemplifies the idealized success of the citizen's deal which has nothing to do with expanded union representation and protection, guaranteed increase in living wages, pensions, and health care, it is characterized as individualist success commercially embodied as a representative of an essentially meaningless industry and its commodity:

> the traumatized role
>
> was the big breakthrough
>
> for the actor
>
> landing him
>
> a 'new fragrance' deal (442)

Solt's poetry makes no claim to a synthesis with the ego and its transcendental qualifiers exacting personal meaning, a lament over its absence, or a "distorted" entrenchment of significance in the face of our economical, ecological, and racially brutalized reality. Not including clandestine corporate polluting, exploitation, or military aggression that goes unreported, the speaker of his poems born in a century of unprecedented massacres, decimation of species, overall environmental destruction, portrays the common life, experiences, and fantasies of a world citizen anticipating the build-up to an inevitable catastrophe in the twenty-first century.

However affected by the twentieth century's world wars and war in general against the international working class, we regularly find the sensibility of erotic, mystical, or shamanistic contemplation in the

majority of poets, including those most influential to the post-WWII generation: for example, Kenneth Rexroth, George Oppen, Allen Ginsberg, Adrienne Rich, Robert Bly, Denise Levertov, Gary Snyder, at times evoke a life of erotic and mystical experiences resisting a personal perplexity or melancholy, resulting in a merging with being. Nature and reciprocity. It is not evasive, but a necessary self-healing reclusion behind the radical humane social consciousness of many poets. Jack Hirschman and Ernesto Cardenal are examples of trenchantly "undistorted" poets. Solt is closer to Nicanor Parra, radical but comical. Anti-poets.

Rexroth, Snyder, Mary Oliver, Antonio Machado, generally most artists and poets, favor the contemplative resolve. Solt resists. It is not a matter of knowing better, or that he discredits moments of transcendence, it is a matter of temperament, an act of non-idealization, frustration as an absurdly livable condition. No valor in either direction. Temperament is not a one-dimensional fate. "undistorted" does not mean fulfilled, or unfulfilled. There is, however, a sense of non-idealizing affirmation in several of his poems; for example, in "glasses," dedicated to Ira Cohen:

glasses

i am visiting

at midnight

full moon

july

what is in store for me?

howling?

akashic wandering?

subterranean jackaling?

we have the leaves

you alone have the flower

it was none of the above

and more

so good to see you

working again

in underwear

sweat dripping off

prism monocle

stuck to your third eye

lost in a subway years ago

that machine is still running

through your shimmering mirror

of heavens and hells

bless your donut earlobes! (184-186)

Fantasy is a value in that moment when it is, in fact, more than surreal. The surreal images in Solt's "what is in store for me? / howling? / akashic wandering? / subterranean jackaling?" are not only related to himself, but to the presence of the poem's recipient, the poet-photographer Ira Cohen, known and adulated by some for his tall-tale monologic intensity, surrealist poetry, photography, and film. The images disperse into a portrait of emotional impression fraught with excited distress, but the authority causing distress in the speaker's mind, Cohen, the only possessor of the "flower," becomes deflated and elevated by the paradox that the "midnight" experience "was none of the above / and more." The poem is a convincing ode to Ira Cohen and his artistic construction "machine...still running/ through [his] shimmering mirror/ of heavens and hells" (186).

Poems for the Unborn is a unique production overall; one crucial factor: nothing has been spared in the high quality of the book's hardcover production. Another factor of its originality: all the poems appeared over a thirty-year period in the Japanese poetry journal, *gui*; over three-hundred pages of poetry in English with translations into Japanese (the bilingual edition is 702 pages). Additionally, there is an absorbing introduction to the book by the translator Aoki Eiko. Aside from her translating concerns, there are brief astute commentaries on the qualities of the poems and their originality. In particular, following the necessary biographical background, she astutely comments on Solt's "peculiar absurdist humor to probe human darkness and the depths of consciousness" (685). Aoki also notes the relief of not being subjected to the canonical tradition of "romantic and lost-love poetry," or "confessions about inner anxieties." She refers to the following comic-erotic poem as an example:

> the run in your stocking
>
> tears through my head
>
> popping my third eye
>
> open in a fever

Of course, she's right about his "surrealist mindset." Earlier in the book, a strong example of his erotic non-derivative surrealism occurs on page 384:   you opened your mind

    like your legs

    only much slower

    better ecstasy

    than never

    hydrangea

    on a zebra

    i put my ear

    to the river

    you put a seashell

    to yours

    you hear

    what i feel

    below moaning wind

    one bird as afterthought

In language, fantasy, the fundamental organ of creative vitality, should extend realism, often by disrupting anticipation and expectation, even to the point of an imponderable probability, a retelling of realism, as in the prose poems of Max Jacob and Russel Edson, and the poems of Kitasono Katue who Solt has translated in an edition of selected poems. The organ of fantasy complexifies realism, as dreams extend or footnote the actual qualities of personality and experience, asserting additional complexity.

The elements of Cubism, Collage, Photomontage, Anti-Poetry, Dada, Surrealism, Magical Realism, and the origination of Plastic Poems (Kitasono's photographic hybrid invention), will continue to display the fact there is no single determiner for meaning, especially through traditional signs and signifiers, the reductive sapped-out artifice of traditional metaphor. Like many of the poems in this book, John Solt's "Glasses" poem, and the paradox that concludes it, presents a sensation of de ja vu, the too often lost value of an experience of de ja vu. As meaning. Undistorted. Historically inclusive in our human traditions:

> the family portrait:

> genetically beat up (376).

Doren Robbins' poetry and poetic prose monologues have appeared in many periodicals, including *The American Poetry Review, Cimarron Review, 5 AM, Hotel Amerika, The Indiana Review, The Iowa Review, Kayak, Lana Turner, Los Angeles Weekly, Nimrod, and Sulfur;* selections of his art have appeared in *Another Chicago Magazine, Agave, Angry Old Man, Caliban, Cholla Needles, Club Plum, Empty Mirror, The Houston Literary Review, Moon and Sun, Otoliths, Paterson Museum of Art (writers that are artists exhibition), Pensive, Ranger, SULΦUR surrealist jungle, Red Wheelbarrow, Third Rail Journal of the Arts, Utriculi,* and in *The Ontological Museum New Acquisitions Catalog,* and others.

Past collections of his poetry and poetic prose monologues *Driving Face Down* and *My Piece of the Puzzle* were awarded **the Blue Lynx Poetry Award 2001** and **the 2008 PEN Oakland Josephine Miles Poetry Award**, respectively. His book *Twin Extra: A Poem in Three Parts* from Wild Ocean Press was **nominated for the Jewish National Book Council Award in Poetry**. In 2021 Spuyten Duyvil Press published *Sympathetic Manifesto, Selected Poems 1975-2015.*

Out of Print. In 2025, Sandy Press will publish his book *Itinerant Dreamer*, a collage of genres (84 art works with related poems and essays). He taught literature and creative writing at Foothill College 2001-2022. Professor Emeritus 2017-2022.

Eileen Tabios

Chants from "The Diasporic Engkanto's Diary"

Chant #1,000,010

Remember the chateau
where you and I never slept

but compromised for a tango?
Velvet blackened my breasts.

You demanded velvet despite the heat
for an image lacking the immortality

of a holiday postcard scene amidst
stone ruins and gawking villagers.

Your glance seared my thigh lifted in
a disguise called "tango." Nothing hapless

about a broken crown. Eldest sons, when
royal, are meant to be broken lest

they never become human. Ach!
The author got it wrong and fiction

does not provide an excuse.
Birds don't chatter from fig tree

canopies. Simply, birds part beaks
to stab then eat the damn figs! Certain

things are meant to be split—things
that are too histrionic to avoid over

-ripeness are meant to be eaten
mercilessly. Because you would not

partake, you fueled my wings. *Damn
your honor*, proclaims this ingrate.

Chant #1,000,015

I lied. Sometimes, *my* midnights do
not cancel the stars. Or

moon, whose liquid light reeks
of nymph lilies, steeled by motes

of green leaf tobacco. Should I
reveal the significance to how

I know the difference between the scent
of cigar boxes and dewed leaves

helpless against aphids in boiling fields?
I could say, "I am the expatriated

daughter of tobacco farmers." You
would hear, "I can be myself

only in exile." Another old story.
Pshaw—just a myth even, insolently reminds

a cartoon character poking its head
onto the bottom of this page. How to know

if I've indeed betrayed a country
whose weather is unsatisfactory. Where

I come from, the air is usually over
-heated: a tiresome virgin to lovely fog.

Chant #1,000,047

We plunged straight into the dark
-est part of the clouds. Years

later I will recall this night
as despair for realizing: the only

sources of light were guns
expelling bullets. Stars hid

to block *Ascencion*. An empty
tomb still waited for its

occupant before an ever-vigilant
servant would lean shoulders

against a boulder to block
the entrance and exit to a cave.

Lord, they have never stopped
needing You. Why was I sent?

My story is that I fell to discover
my vision instead of inherited sight.

But you whose wounded eyes
mirror mine (though against my

will), why did you blacken my
wings? I loathe martyrdom.

I loathe sacrifice. I loathe my
unexpected mor(t)ality for having

fallen in love with one of them—
this gloriously benighted race for

whom some matter is always
infected with pain, and contagious.

Chants #1,000,040 and #1,000,033

No medicine for *this* by changing
its name from *Loneliness*. We both ran

like masters from rebellious slaves. I mis-
judged direction while you gauged with

precision. You also foretold accurately:
the stars will not speak of me while you

look at them from the island of Mallorca.
Such is the healing hue of which gold

also is capable. On Mallorca, to see
is to observe children build fences

with the same rhythm contained in the stone
-hard muscles of shepherds and fishermen.

Never should barbed wire extend
against the blue of an ocean.

A silver wink suffices to crack light
and leave a legacy of scarring color.

Memory, too, can commit
sins in the inhuman realm.

The strength of the intangible
is how no shield against it can defend.

See how winter light brings a distasteful
grey film that coats everything, even those hiding?

Chant #1,000,052

So, bright angel, hold my hand.
Let's turn "everything" into abstract

background to the foreground of our
escape. *A fire burns in the ice*

cave. She says, "I want this
pain." Engkanto says, "I know you

want this pain." She says, "I
long to be a tree in a hurricane.

Uprooted, I finally would fly!"
Angel says, "You want this pain."

Eileen R. Tabios has released books of poetry, fiction, essays, art and experimental prose around the world. Publications include the novel *The Balikbayan Artist*; an art monograph *Drawing Six Directions;* a poetry collection *Because I Love You, I Become War*; an autobiography, *The Inventor;* and a flash fiction collection (with harry k stammer), *Getting To One.* Her books have been translated into Filipino, French, Spanish, Thai and Romanian; other writings have been translated into Binisaya, Russian, Bengal, Japanese, Portuguese, Italian, Polish, and Greek. More information at https://eileenrtabios.com

Robert Beveridge

Banana Milkshake

you awake from a nap
and discover the house
has burned down.
you wonder
if the peanut butter
made it through
unscathed

Dalmation

—it is the hole
and how the hole
is dug (or how
we dig the hole)

and the door—

*

archway under
the hill with all
the valuables
inside.

*

You prepare tea
from the stones
you carved away
to make this place

from the leaves
of the trees

29

from the wool
of the animals
outside

rounded
full of chicory
thyme, velocity,
force and mass

and endless ocean.

*

I am still outside
and I put my feet
where they seem
to need to be
to enter

and yet I stand
three feet above
the ground

thirsty

Exit Smiling

I kiss you in this ancient world
where all the white sand beneath our feet
has been replaced with iron filings

and the sound of birds in the trees
has been replaced with the sound
of lathes and the chisels
and the knurls

but what does it matter?
Perhaps you too find these noises pleasant

have you eaten?

Panama

Scorn mocks
the eyes of the scarred
asphyxiated lovers litter
yellow streets

awakened yellow-eyed beast
walks unfettered
                        survivors
afraid cower from its
yellow contagious breath

fingers clench jaws
rip the bodies
of the diseased
meat yellows at death

disease-beast strikes at random
ravages cities, villages,
scars survivors for life
takes loved and unloved
evil and good
                    shows
neither favor nor mercy

Rotten

The yellow and black stripes

ground zero

the necessity of eyedrops
and the optional earlobes

pizza folded into an origami swan

an asteroid on its way

Robert Beveridge (he/him) makes noise
(xterminal.bandcamp.com) and writes poetry on unceded Mingo
land (Akron, OH). He published his first poem in a non-
vanity/non-school publication in November 1988, and it's been all
downhill since. Recent/upcoming appearances in Gypsophila,
Failed Haiku, and Wordpeace, among others.

Social Media:
MeWe: https://mewe.com/xterminal.56/posts
Letterboxd: https://letterboxd.com/xterminal/
last.fm: https://www.last.fm/user/xterminal

Mark Young

Four Tom Beckett Titles

Forgotten Fantasies

"*I was saved by doG to make America grate again.*" — D. J. T.®.

Annie Leibovitz once sought me out to pose for a *Rolling Stone* cover photo wearing only an orange thong.

Barack Obama wanted to come on to *The Apprentice*. He didn't make it past the first screen test. "You're fired!" I told him.

Chelsea Manning was my late night hornpipe-dream until I discovered they weren't the Clinton's daughter.

Donald Jr. upheld his pledge for the family trust to not do deals & investments in foreign countries, as well as not collect payments from foreign governments in its U.S. properties, during my first term in office.

Europe willingly became my fiefdom.

Fans flocked to the T.®umpcon I arranged at the Capitol Building in 2021.

Gerontologists predict that I'm going to live longer than Methuselah.

Haitians lined up in droves to pay homage to me, believing I was the Messiah. I gave visas to those who brought a benison. The remainder begged for beneficence. I don't know what the words mean.

Israelis also believe I'm the Mashiach, the Messiah. I've given them Lebanon & Syria already, & tomorrow when I wake, I'm going to give them Mesopotamia & Persia. I love those old-fashioned names!

Next week I'm giving them the Ukraine & China because those countries are going to cost me money & the I.D.F. knows how to handle uppity countries.

Jack Black wanted to falsely indict me for trying to overturn the 2020 election results. I took his Emmy away.

Kelloggs have begun to include T.®ump figurines in their Corn Flakes packets. Anyone who collects twenty of them will be guaranteed a spot in Heaven because, by then, I'll be the centerpiece of the Trinity.

"Let me grab your pussy," I say to every woman I find attractive who I come in contact with & they let me.

Melania doesn't get pissed at me.

"Nearer my God to thee," shout the adoring crowds pressing closer as I pass through them.

Overseas military service is something I would have willingly participated in, but my country needed me elsewhere.

Papa Was a Rollin' Stone was one of the first singles I released. My version made it to No. 1 on the *Billboard* Hot 100.

Queer Theory, as I have often stated, is the philosophy that binds my administration together.

Rand Paul said, in September of 2014, "The President, Barack Obama, acts like he's a king." I've decided to go one step better & proclaim myself one.

Society needs me as an unbiased arbiter. No one else in the world

could fill such a role.

Teleprompters are something I do not need. I write my own
speeches, remember them, & speak them without notes.
United the States had never been until I came along.

Vladimir Putin has permanently canceled Russia's Victory Parades
because he knows they can't compare to mine. Mine's bigger &
better in every respect.

Weltherrschaft, world domination, is not something that the
Elongated Muskrat & I are deliberately seeking. But should it
happen, we both have the ethical & moral fortitude not to take
advantage of it.

X has tried to maintain its pace with my Truth Social but can't keep
up. It's no contest. See V above.

You only have to see my oversize & illegible & arrogant Sharpied
signature on the plethora of executive orders I have executed to
know that I'm a man of wealth & taste.

Zelenskyy is a pain in my rectum. When I have a spare afternoon,
I'm going to paint him pink, parcel him up, & sell him to the
highest bidder.

Ghost Whirl

There aren't many choices in
the context of real music per-
formance now that the bug
category has been changed to
critical & white shapes illumi-
nate the village bakery. Some-
thing went wrong while

submitting the form. Lyrics
for the song have yet to be
transcribed. Nightmare fuel
cells have exploded & set the
transcriber alight in a true pad-
dock-to-plate experience. The
only functioning things left are

rhythms composed of simple
integer ratios, & a mathematical
function that extracts a character
or a specific number of characters
from a text string. As technology
develops, the lines the mind per-
ceives become increasingly faint.

Homopho...ights

Five m... ...fter I
...se into
plug...I partner
G... & tells
...it's *knights*.
...ge there for a
...ried I may
...d in some-
could have
...ne morality
...round. But now
...reathing easier, I
...urn to Google &
enter 'homophobe
knights' which is what
I was going to search
for in the first place,
to see if the castle
cloisters were safe for
a struggling minstrel
to stay in overnight.

Irregular Interventions

Apparently influenced by the concept
of Manifest Destiny, a dominant theme
in the history is a subculture of birds
made queer by endocrine disruptors.

It's a pervasive idea, a form of colon-
ial environmental violence, worked
around an exhaustive dataset of cells
that limit the entry of race into popu-

lations. A supervised machine learn-
ing model to predict pipeline success
in which it is remarkable should a
middle/passive verb occur even twice.

Mark Young was born in Aotearoa / New Zealand but now lives
in a small town in North Queensland in Australia. He has been
publishing poetry for over sixty-five years, & is the author of
around seventy-five books, primarily text poetry but also including
speculative fiction, vispo, non-fiction, & art history. His most
recent books are *Some Unrecorded Voyages of Vasco da Gama*,
from Otoliths, Home Hill, Australia; the downloadable pdf, *Closed
Environment*, from Neo-Mimeo Editions, Nualláin House, Monte
Rio, California, U.S.A; & *The Complete Post Person Poems*, from
Sandy Press, all published in March 2025.

Eric Lunde

OND SECOND DARK AGE
THF

ond dark age
I(m Sunday or any day
y is dead
Ghost-dance rite. Tepid
nd dark age, the Fall)

comes up on you from the back a shade of its serf
f and grill power up that downsized hill
comes up from behind sneaks in the dowdy floral arrangement
And announces it kilter, in place, ajar, akimbo.
A second to live in the second second dark age
Its medieval in these sand traps!
I have a tingle for a bosch fire bird shaped doctor article
Articulate in the grime
No one tells you when they will turn the lights out.
It just dials down and you wake up alone with your
Shivers and Cormac McCarthy.
A funnel on your gulliver doesn't make you king
But you might as well act the part
Because in the dark no one knows
Even that god there spurned by hirsute florists
Under siege from the plague
a pocketful of Dillingers will circle round,
Move them to the side what odors dreamed up by
Mythical figurines in the menagerie….
A fidget of lizards a grim of insects
Who is this playing a lute on my shining brow?
Bagpipes on your head? De rigueur! Tres chic!
Just don't play them in front of the mirror.
Second of a second dark age a sliver of a shiver.
In the silver glitter of the screen
The Medici lives amongst us a
disparate band of unrelated torsos

funk of money and
Musk of radar equipped with signaling devices
What's the next act? What follows the dog?

Indentured servitude has little to do with teeth
But you'd sell them for a turnip
A quick trepanning and you're good to go!
Let's talk about them Hellenic ass fuckers and pederast!
No he said he was a podiatrist!
Straight outta Lausanne! M. C. Escher drew this city,
You are going up as you go down!
That's more like it! Keep the faith! He drawled….
There's a dark age every second you just can't keep up.
You with the Funnel!
Remove these stones from our heads!

A bubble emerging from the cricket's mouth
Becomes a bulb to store virgins in.

The sun in palindrome
Apollopa! The god of the same difference!
It does commute the same reverse
Spells the light emitted so….
Bosch out in the crowd! Someone give him a camera!
We're under the heavy hand of the
Juiced influencer, posting her schedule of dress
Appointments, tresses, a greeting card homily
Nothing ventured nothing wept.
Here come the fires distant and stout
Punctuating the horizon…

WE TAKE GHOSTS

The sign said we take ghosts
So I paid them in ghosts   a long arduous process
Of taking out the machinery
And press each ghost out
And present them to the cashier….
ghost
Is currency as it rends holes in the
past and crowds out the present…
I bought a lamp, seven cans of tinned meat and
A spool of red thread. see
If you get change back
You have to tie the loose ghosts
Together….

I USED TO LIKE THIS PLACE UNTIL THEY MADE ALL THESE RENOVATIONS

It is a dark respite   residue, familiar   without aboutface
Turn.   .   . what clock is this time coming from? ???
Surely not this one   held fast to the wall with glue   it has not been
Updated since they made   ALL THESE RENOVATIONS.

       .   .
Time.   Stops when it wants to or
Depletes the batteries..   . there was a time
When I had feeling   in my legs I   miss not being here
I want to not care about the things that are gone
But here we are   SO   sue me ..   .
There used to be a chute   here   >
to slide all the debris collected   away from you
into absence   forgotten until collected by
the waste collection company.   After which it is
out of your control   what happens to
the things parted from.   I wish I had this option a
chute for memory.   .   .   … Maybe
NOW you'll believe me this place was better

Before they made all these renovations.

I USED TO LIKE THIS PLACE UNTIL THEY MADE ALL THESE RENOVATIONS

First of all there is this   venal hue of beige
And the flourish of orange roughy color scheme in every follicle
on
His head right   ??? the costs reflected in the selection
Of stackable polypropylene   chairs
for good measure they brought in
Rolls of sod to embellish the   course with.
Everyone holds a flag everyone runs the skirmish everyone
Runs…   .   . possibly I could get used to this

RAT PATTERN

WHAT ever is that message shadowed out on whittle walls granite
sweating internally
Say that with me Rat is peony pattern everything ditches sent to
Intercepted from
Midair catch by raw hand teethed
razor oblivion necromantic year
puzzled look scurvy and act facetious
you'll make hang from their bloviations!

ITS OUT OF YOUR HANDS

Homophone Nights

Five minutes after I
plug the phrase into
Google, its AI partner
comes awake & tells
me it thinks it's *knights*.
I was on edge there for a
while, worried I may
have keyed in some-
thing that could have
brought the morality
police around. But now
I'm breathing easier, I
return to Google &
enter 'homophobe
knights' which is what
I was going to search
for in the first place,
to see if the castle
cloisters were safe for
a struggling minstrel
to stay in overnight.

Irregular Interventions

Apparently influenced by the concept
of Manifest Destiny, a dominant theme
in the history is a subculture of birds
made queer by endocrine disruptors.

It's a pervasive idea, a form of colon-
ial environmental violence, worked
around an exhaustive dataset of cells
that limit the entry of race into popu-

lations. A supervised machine learn-
ing model to predict pipeline success
in which it is remarkable should a
middle/passive verb occur even twice.

Mark Young was born in Aotearoa / New Zealand but now lives
in a small town in North Queensland in Australia. He has been
publishing poetry for over sixty-five years, & is the author of
around seventy-five books, primarily text poetry but also including
speculative fiction, vispo, non-fiction, & art history. His most
recent books are *Some Unrecorded Voyages of Vasco da Gama*,
from Otoliths, Home Hill, Australia; the downloadable pdf, *Closed
Environment*, from Neo-Mimeo Editions, Nualláin House, Monte
Rio, California, U.S.A; & *The Complete Post Person Poems*, from
Sandy Press, all published in March 2025.

Eric Lunde

THE SECOND SECOND DARK AGE

It's a second dark age
No Psalm Sunday or any day
The city is dead
Bust. Ghost-dance rite. Tepid
(second dark age, the Fall)

IT comes up on you from the back a shade of its serf
Oaf and grill power up that downsized hill
It comes up from behind sneaks in the dowdy floral arrangement
And announces it kilter, in place, ajar, akimbo.
A second to live in the second second dark age
Its medieval in these sand traps!
I have a tingle for a bosch fire bird shaped doctor article
Articulate in the grime
No one tells you when they will turn the lights out.
It just dials down and you wake up alone with your
Shivers and Cormac McCarthy.
A funnel on your gulliver doesn't make you king
But you might as well act the part
Because in the dark no one knows
Even that god there spurned by hirsute florists
Under siege from the plague
 a pocketful of Dillingers will circle round,
Move them to the side what odors dreamed up by
Mythical figurines in the menagerie....
A fidget of lizards a grim of insects
Who is this playing a lute on my shining brow?
Bagpipes on your head? De rigueur! Tres chic!
Just don't play them in front of the mirror.
Second of a second dark age a sliver of a shiver.
In the silver glitter of the screen
The Medici lives amongst us a
disparate band of unrelated torsos

funk of money and
Musk of radar equipped with signaling devices
What's the next act? What follows the dog?

Indentured servitude has little to do with teeth
But you'd sell them for a turnip
A quick trepanning and you're good to go!
Let's talk about them Hellenic ass fuckers and pederast!
No he said he was a podiatrist!
Straight outta Lausanne! M. C. Escher drew this city,
You are going up as you go down!
That's more like it! Keep the faith! He drawled....
There's a dark age every second you just can't keep up.
You with the Funnel!
Remove these stones from our heads!

A bubble emerging from the cricket's mouth
Becomes a bulb to store virgins in.

The sun in palindrome
Apollopa! The god of the same difference!
It does commute the same reverse
Spells the light emitted so....
Bosch out in the crowd! Someone give him a camera!
We're under the heavy hand of the
Juiced influencer, posting her schedule of dress
Appointments, tresses, a greeting card homily
Nothing ventured nothing wept.
Here come the fires distant and stout
Punctuating the horizon...

WE TAKE GHOSTS

The sign said we take ghosts
So I paid them in ghosts   a long arduous process
Of taking out the machinery
And press each ghost out
And present them to the cashier….
ghost
Is currency as it rends holes in the
past and crowds out the present…
I bought a lamp, seven cans of tinned meat and
A spool of red thread. see
If you get change back
You have to tie the loose ghosts
Together….

I USED TO LIKE THIS PLACE UNTIL THEY MADE ALL THESE RENOVATIONS

It is a dark respite   residue, familiar   without aboutface
Turn. .   . what clock is this time coming from? ???
Surely not this one   held fast to the wall with glue   it has not been
Updated since they made   ALL THESE RENOVATIONS.

                .   .

Time.   Stops when it wants to or
Depletes the batteries..   . there was a time
When I had feeling   in my legs I   miss not being here
I want to not care about the things that are gone
But here we are   SO   sue me ..   .
There used to be a chute   here   >
to slide all the debris collected   away from you
into absence   forgotten until collected by
the waste collection company.   After which it is
out of your control   what happens to
the things parted from.   I wish I had this option a
chute for memory.   .   .   … Maybe
NOW you'll believe me this place was better

Before they made all these renovations.

I USED TO LIKE THIS PLACE UNTIL THEY MADE ALL
THESE RENOVATIONS

First of all there is this   venal hue of beige
And the flourish of orange roughy color scheme in every follicle
on
His head right   ??? the costs reflected in the selection
Of stackable polypropylene   chairs
for good measure they brought in
Rolls of sod to embellish the   course with.
Everyone holds a flag everyone runs the skirmish everyone
Runs…   .   . possibly I could get used to this

RAT PATTERN

WHAT ever is that message shadowed out on whittle walls granite
sweating internally
Say that with me Rat is peony pattern everything ditches sent to
Intercepted from
Midair catch by raw hand teethed
razor oblivion necromantic year
puzzled look scurvy and act facetious
you'll make hang from their bloviations!

ITS OUT OF YOUR HANDS

PAYWALL

You can be so much flame when
I had bounce in to…
Perchance you mentioned me in the article?
A hard no will suffice

DOVES   CROWDS   BANDAGES
         yyy   e   t   ….
No, no one I point to will hold you to that
UNLESS EXCHANGED
One hand beckons to the other
                           No, how?
Your right. One hand coerces the other
Intruding on this read until the path
Is leased and the access granted first your money
Then your life and you can get
Down to the anxiety you're all
Ready practiced at
Well versed in
Professionally speaking…..

Eric Lunde lives in Minneapolis MN USA. With many years of engagement in the arts, he has worked in audio art, performance, spoken word. He has numerous audio releases to his name. He also self-publishes poetry, theory, and graphic work. He works on his own line of block ink printed works under the imprint Kanshiketsu! which includes postcards and mail art, handmade books, prints. "To me life is a long stutter with occasional beneficial accidents. There are moments of clarity and then there's interference. Words, I don't think, should be spared from this routine, this pattern. And if anything, language is the perfect place to celebrate and engage in this condition." Work can be viewed and purchased at the following :
https://kanshiketsu.substack.com/
https://endythekid.blogspot.com/
https://kanshiketsu.bandcamp.com/
https://www.lulu.com/spotlight/lunde

K.S. Ernst Sheila & E. Murphy

#52

Regard this moonlight bird song
Bejeweled with seeds and feathers
Too far from here to feel
Then whisper as a mood goes by

Song accompanied by eyes
Sheathed in parentheses
Picture pure refraction
Held in mind lifts

What's been here a while
Now settled on another way
Midnight moon pays the price
For blue patches in the morning

Allowing a release from habit
And routine maintained
Along familiar pathways
In time to mean the simplest things

112

Who needs cobblestones? Perhaps those little sparrows that
Scavenge for seeds in the cracks then vanish suddenly
Into the blooming bushes. And as for us
Alert new breezes keep our eyes attending

To a bluer blue and the occasional cloud shred.
Fullness or emptiness, what's the difference?
Maybe volume, maybe something weighable.
Look at the brown feathers chameleon themselves into safety.

What I picture when I picture you is a vast and generous
woodland.
How many deer sneak past without being seen?
And the mood birds, how many are there, and what notes?
And do they have all the seeds they need?

#122

A humming sound, a blaze of breeze,
A chirp, a cheep from birds above,
branches from here appear firm
if unsheathed in their moving.
Leaves stroke one another
Some of the leaflings still hinged
give way to thinking music into them.
And lithe mimicry in the body opens the way
to a little contagion of the simple pleasure
of anything alive.

126

If past is pasture beyond the last left turn
you're new only to this feathered mist once listless
simile: like Joan dashing among taxis
cashless but look she has a card
metaphor: a bat gliding for a ride
now frayed forward toward north
now heading forth to
where feeble shells revive smells
of feathered creatures never born
where shore weathered across seasons
supplies reasons duly hatched
patched with imagined magic
flails from coincidence derailed
to secrets held unshared while
spared white space across beneath beyond
apace a mind-free fare (taxi)

128

Miniature golf on carpet concrete or turf
A red ball gleams in the scrubby bushes
Miniature gold as in Daniel Brush
Traces of golden dust on the fleece
Miniature limber limbs transcending tree limbs
Quench lingering laughter
Miniature falsetto crunching glass
From fingertips and bleeding thumb
Miniature frost against the brittle window
Shapeshifting forth and back
Miniature windows geometric as parks
Or as cards drawn to detect a door
Miniature glow of golden yearning for years
And years and years that seemed profound
Miniature notation on miniature parchment
Slanted disappointment thus drawn down
Miniature composition retrieving the world in another time
Devising a way to undermine the whole
Miniature roses in a row receiving sprinkler water
Betting against yesterday on a windblown day

K.S. Ernst likes to get her hands on her words so she frequently uses three-dimensional letters to create mixed media pieces. Much of her work is painted, collaged, or created by drawing on the computer. In addition to appearing in literary magazines her pieces are often exhibited in galleries, museums, and libraries. Books include *Drop Cap* and *Sequencing:* (both from Xexoxial Editions) and *The Last Vispo Anthology* (Fantagraphics). Books with Sheila E. Murphy are *Permutoria* and *Underscore* (Luna Bisonte Prods) and *2 Juries + 2 Storeys = 4 Stories Toujours* (Xexoxial Editions). Sites housing substantial collections of Ernst's work are Ohio State University Avant Garde and Experimental Writing Collection; The Poetry Collection of the University Libraries, University at Buffalo; and Yale University's Beinecke Rare Book and Manuscript Library. Website: www.ksernst.com.

Sheila E. Murphy Appeared in *Verse Daily, Fortnightly Review, Poetry, Hanging Loose,* and others. Most recent book: *Escritoire* (Lavender Ink, 2025). Won the Gertrude Stein Poetry Award for *Letters to Unfinished J.* (Green Integer Press, 2003). Won the Hay(ha)ku Book Prize for *Reporting Live From You Know Where* (Meritage Press, 2018). She lives in Phoenix, Arizona.
Her Wikipedia page can be found at:
https://en.wikipedia.org/wiki/Sheila_Murphy

BÍRÓ JÓZSEF

SUPREMATIST POEM

(1)

feketén feketefeketénfeketefeketénfekete
feketénfeketefeketénfeketefeketénfekete
feketénfeketefeketénfeketefeketénfekete
feketénfeketefeketénfeketefeketénfekete
feketénfeketefeketénfeketefeketénfekete
feketénfeketefeketénfeketefeketénfekete
feketénfeketefeketénfeketefeketénfekete
feketénfeketefeketénfeketefeketénfekete
feketénfeketefeketénfeketefeketénfekete
feketénfeketefeketénfeketefeketénfekete
feketénfeketefeketénfeketefeketénfekete
feketénfeketefeketénfeketefeketénfekete

fehérfeketefeketefehérfehérfekete

fehérfehérenfehérfehérenfehérfehéren
fehérfehérenfehérfehérenfehérfehéren
fehérfehérenfehérfehérenfehérfehéren
fehérfehérenfehérfehérenfehérfehéren
fehérfehérenfehérfehérenfehérfehéren
fehérfehérenfehérfehérenfehérfehéren
fehérfehérenfehérfehérenfehérfehéren
fehérfehérenfehérfehérenfehérfehéren
fehérfehérenfehérfehérenfehérfehéren
fehérfehérenfehérfehérenfehérfehéren
fehérfehérenfehérfehérenfehérfehéren

fehérfehérenfehérfehérenfehér *fehéren*

VÖRÖSFEHÉRFEHÉRVÖRÖSVÖRÖSFEHÉR

vörös fehérenvörösfehérenvörösfehéren
vörösfehérenvörösfehérenvörösfehéren
vörösfehérenvörösfehérenvörösfehéren
vörösfehérenvörösfehérenvörösfehéren
vörösfehérenvörösfehérenvörösfehéren
vörösfehérenvörösfehérenvörös *fehéren*
vörös fehérenvörösfehérenvörösfehéren
vörösfehérenvörösfehérenvörösfehéren
vörösfehérenvörösfehérenvörösfehéren
vörösfehérenvörösfehérenvörösfehéren
vörösfehérenvörösfehérenvörösfehéren
vörösfehérenvörösfehérenvörös *fehéren*

FEHÉRVÖRÖSVÖRÖSFEHÉRFEHÉRVÖRÖS

(in remembrance of Kazimir Malevich)

SUPREMATIST POEM

(2)

black whitewhiteblack
whiteblackblackwhite
blackwhitewhiteblack
whiteblackblackwhite
blackwhitewhiteblack
whiteblackblackwhite
blackwhitewhiteblack
whiteblackblackwhite
blackwhitewhite *black*

whitered redwhite whitered   redwhite whitered redwhite
redwhite whitered redwhite   whitered redwhite whitered
whitered redwhite whitered   redwhite whitered redwhite
redwhite whitered redwhite   whitered redwhite whitered
whitered redwhite white *red*   red *white* whitered redwhite
redwhite whitered redwhite   whitered redwhite whitered
whitered redwhite whitered   redwhite whitered redwhite
redwhite whitered redwhite   whitered redwhite whitered
whitered redwhite withered   redwhite whitered redwhite

black whitewhiteblack
whiteblackblackwhite
blackwhitewhiteblack
whiteblackblackwhite
blackwhitewhiteblack

whiteblackblackwhite
blackwhitewhiteblack
whiteblackblackwhite
blackwhitewhite *black*

(in remembrance of Kazimir Malevich)

SUPREMATIST POEM

(3)

JÓZSEF BÍRÓ

(- poet / writer / visual artist / performer ... and sometimes editor -)

JÓZSEF BÍRÓ was born in 19 may 1951 / BUDAPEST / HUNGARY
poet – writer – visual artist and performer 1975 to present
organizational memberships : Hungarian Alliance of Writers
/ Art Foundation of Hungarian Republic / Belletrist Assotiation /
Nine Dragon Heads International Artist Group – (South – Korea
) / *etc.*

published works : 41 books and booklets (1986 – 2025)

creative works :

9 individual exhibitions
more than 700 group exhibitions around the world
more than 90 single (live) – performances around the world

hungarian prizes :

HUNGARIAN GOLD CROSS OF MERIT

RECOGNITION OF ARTISTIC OUVRE

ATTILA JÓZSEF – PRIZE

Joshua Martin

Let the false Alarms meander in the Borrowed Puffs

waning   hUm:
   burden of hieroglyphic hammers:
 >, once becomes a blank-faced kimono,
   then a Farewell hOOd,
  index finger plums = = =
      FaMiLy
      MoVeMenT
      ViRuS,
   [fantasy pigeon coffee breaks]
> , > , > ,
   ciphers (fretting vegetative state of the union
        SHRIEKING!!!!!) =>
  => =>
  | plain, just because graphic sutures
  offer aberrations & almost fluttering
  schemes (bare? neutral? sprouting?)
  imprisoned, a perverse plaid snow
  snoozing artichoke slivers as a study
  in hand-tinted harmony | <= <= <=
lEAks
SPRUNG diabolical quarantine
      shoelace zeppelin >!<,
  not enough worrying
  eruptions: it SHOT
     massaged latches =>,
 pilgrim, headphones, morphed babel!,
   ?fully hunched?
 marbles swiftly as in a sprained
 lemon toaster slat:
     screen door rhyme,
     during a squared
     bash, an acceleration
     told as if an antique
     quotation . . . .

pepper spray
as an apparent peapod laughing fit=
enormous items
[bizarre factors,
ridges,
#ed shelves of Egyptian
rebukes = TaX oN
A SPIDER=
WEB
dingbat > , => => =>
pray,
STURDY flashbacks modestly
slurred & carrots:
| absorbed gates of stationary store ducks
> bills / phantoms / quivering headlong in/
to corpulent sketches < : 'the best a ladder
could EveR achieve IN SWEEP=ING &
b/l/a/n/d roly-poly ants (a vase? an album
without aluminum?) sausage blankets >
meat smudge > afloat! swiftly ! = ! = ! = ?
differed, enough rectangular divisions of
labor = ? = ? = ? = ? = ? = ? = ? = ? = ? =
tAdPoLe tunnel (deep ridicule vibrations?)
=> => => => => 'what kills the blockage of
toneless lung capacities?' ; How MuCH a
floating sodium garnish hits a sphere | =>
, greatest
striding
PaNtS =
WHAT A RACKET!!!!!
bone,bone,bone,
[little laundering domes of powdered tourism],
NoT
unlike an oxygen
mouthpiece
photographed

             AT THE POINT
                OF
             COLLISION =>=>=>
knees envelope stockyard playwrights
& then the lava reaches our blushing
entrails => =>
                it resembles
                spelling errors,
          though tastes
            of superfluous
                solidifying
                    rainclouds

**under approachable essays, the VoTe an alternative of
outcomes**

                puckered:
    F
    O   O
    U   B   :   gestures
    N   J   :   disguised
    D   E   :   as household
           C   DROOL
           T   >!<,
           S   >?<,
            [movements daunt / daubed
            insect monuments / like
            donut holes blindly based
            On Asphalt = = = = = = = =],
    specialized terrain
    bleeding insecticide SPRINGING,
                    BOUNCING =
            weatherized comparative perspectives
            grown without comparative tissues
            pulling theoretical foundations of
            legalistic jargon / bargains! crusts! / = = =
  s
  h i
  i v

f o l
t r a   collaboration oracles
i y w   drooping,
n   l   impossibilities
g   e   obtaining implicated
       s   morality, straining,
       s   floundering
           with an eyeball
           hagiography TeXtbOOk
                       code:
authorities & privately
authorized /   i
               s   j
               s   u
               u   m
               e   p
               s   i
                  n
               g = = = =
> | commonality, supreme fortress
   of introductory peeling responsibility | < : :
         L
         o   before
         o   scooping
         k   cobweb
                 décor =!=,
usable archival symposiums
       :
         BLAST
            OFF!!!!!!!!!!

Draft Tree Limb Inflation

whirly. foam=ing At The Brink of STAR-BASHING
relegation solidity => => => => whisper feuding pancake
WeaKNeSs : [fuzzy doppelganger rejection NoTePaD schematic] :
: : D=E=V=I=C=E WITH=OUT vestiges of DeePsEa waffle fries
=> =>
   : oF donation vertebrae question mark retaliation :

WEARY CORNHOLE MANHOLE COVER OUTHOUSE

    => => => => =>

> | frolicking attitude re,adjust,ed fumigation half-life
  of refrigerated solitude dustcover fathomless instep
  interior freezer burn cowlick manifesto steroid abuse
  malfunctioning at the speed of manicured helmet
  hair adroit hanky-panky tablature seedling smirk | <
         , : ,
      'Many a maniacal dressing gown
      spinach tossed to and fro while
      withering gurus arrest tired and
      relentlessly fickle pharmacists'
            => ! <=

RAGING SEA MONSTERS ON THE VERGE

    ,

    ,
   , : ; , , ; : : : : :
[blush affectation upheaval drowning
 casino remote control militia cookbook],
    spilling glue,
        contamination water supply
        realities : : : living in

                    wasteful
                    ignorance : :
: :

| ascertaining [must be a kind of plumage?]
  the pitiful and subtle sticks of mangled bells
  \ = un=product=ive saddle burning crystals
  while waging war on shopping habits /=/=/=
  'Whose Afraid of a Little Shivering Undulation?'
  , => => => => (((((that MusT bE An OnioN
  oR at least the verbal cue necessary to ask
  mostly inaudible questions to a mirror image
  of a gorilla costume))))) => => => => => => |

MIRAGE OR BUST

, => => =>,
        GuTLeSS dribbling sewage MasTeR
PuMp,
        in holistic defaults
                    through blushing city wind tunnels
: => :
   [/ !] => => => => => ^ ^ ^ ^ ^,
        energetically damaged while
        a broom placates a nuisance
        horn of plenty smear
                            campaign (,
the last judged occurrence of
                the yearly escape
                awards
        bAsKiNg countless racking of
            the BraiN DeaD => => => =>
glad,
   NoT UN=KNOWN
                bUt scorched underneath
                harmful ideological
                        misery =>)

CURTAIN IN RELENTLESS DESPAIR

eager fan blades offer gestures, homespun diaper maintenance fees, forgettable sunglasses joining baseball bat expiration dates. and what an abysmal state of affairs. sitting. a staid expression of capillary domes seen less as an invention and more as a mangy rehabilitation center publicly reported. searing. which corner office dipshit should be lined up against the wall and deboned? all. insulted affidavit grilling. junk. yards full of ethos, scams, bending in willful disgust to storybook domino effect.

an act of headline, chambered, accumulating under duress

, ergot => deepLY <= an overview drowning subtextual splinter : > 'leanings & drooping phenomenological exertions' < ; ; ; ; ; ! | LiViD aesthetic details circular in as much, later guided = TaUt = frequently an accounting eRRoR (like druid meditation sailboat projectile) = = = ProCeSs beneath radical meaninglessness = = = !, ? , | , = : ; : ; > \ assumed laboratory peculiarities accordingly glum / < = = = ! = = = : hEAl : wild strawberry oceanic parachute publicity machine : \ diatribe of a pinwheel discrepancy MeMbRaNe > > > cryptic beaver fishing rod obliquely delicate < < < : thus, an origin wandering virtually UN=TOUCH=ED : | peace / SHOCK! ! ! ! ! => => => => => Gaseous, decreasing, joyous educational STOP-START-STOP-START-ASCERTAIN | => reductive polyphonic harmony glowing suggested ReTaiL PriCe ; [speech (?) = locomotive metaphysics overturning orientation disease / (SPLATTER tabletop squirting {up! UP!} =) \ ], relay the developmental kinetic scar tissue aggrandizement / = scamper = jangle = fierce vocal FeeDbAcK ethnicity : ensuite = termite = detailed jungle foot awaits your consumer despair:
                , chatting :   cOw
                        hIdE   :
        seeKING   :   thoughtless
                    chimney [a
                            shingle] : bOw,
        spur golden dramaturgy   / / / / / =
(each day
reverses the OTHER) = ! ,

!,
>scrap<, hidden
tRoVeS< [honesty
before

frostbite] / / /

/ / :

'MOODY WHALES CONJURE INACTIVE
FOOTLIGHTS'
/ => => =>
, sullied advice column battery
fingerprinting electricity
pavements:

| have syndrome MaY dRoP pause = select = warning
merchandizing burglary spree intensely a stratagem defined as a
PLaYgRoUnd payCHECK shimmering NON-verbal tabs < 'an
infallible disregard' < : formerly dispersed, uniform, coda, dancing
effective durational iceberg telegraph foam ; ; ; ! taciturn ! flapping
fires, smiling jacket affectation / = pointer, ghostly, MoIsT => > 'is
NoT eNouGh?' < : ShoT, genomes = = = | flightless marketplace,
tying ham-fisted cinders / ALL maximized hydraulic loops strum
milkshake TrAy TaBlE, suffice, S=U=R=F=A=C=E hyperbole
washing machine theory rusted, trotting masked atrium pirouette [a
species, dislocated wincing echo) :::::::::: c,l,a,m,p,e,d aToMic
whoknowswhat :::::::::: => => => => =>
ZiP,
an affectation meme wounded,
betwixt enchilada
hip BoNe => =>,

AGREE TO
DISPERSE ITCHING
LEGACY DEMARCATION =< =< =,
written as velocity pavement > , sudden disconnect < / = hung UP
ON A QuestioN mArK wrinkle = canonical sawdust shingle as
vulnerable as a quixotic monument sinking under the wright of
polluted NeVeR MiNd = plenty
pOUreD, ground
& JuMbO sHrImP

        quilts liberally
     constipated =>
        TrieD => separation of
           EaRtHlY
           rudiments
      drive serenity to the
           brink

Joshua Martin is a Philadelphia based writer and filmmaker, who
currently works in a library. He is a member of C22, an
experimental writing collective. He is the author most recently of
the books Approximate Preparation for Cannibalistic Symphonies
(C22 Press), isolated version of nexus (Pere Ube), and lung
f,r,a,g,m,e,n,t,s before grazing *asterisk* (Moria Poetry). He has
had numerous pieces published in various journals. You can find
links to his published work at joshuamartinwriting.blogspot.com

Sean Meggeson

born

&wire chokes
  device s   2nd thin skin
tape re covers
  red [*i*] dot   mine

fresh memoir   animal cloak
  exposure video
erasure tapes
  translates   cog cold

throw cushion   belly trap
  pike mirror
shards of Buffalo NY
  &ice plants/pants   (shoot crust lullaby)

South of Salamanca
  US 219 ape   picker
burger pretty   >Cage note >[*la*] ready
  lake-effect

Lonnie Liston Smith man
  Jim Hall   (w/ old Spanish blower)
delivery Joes
  &Johnnys reflect   daddy darkness here

j last (to aire

who

could

got

for m)

mini school

relative   t j v   soit and

late   last late rborn   used bare ly see n

ba(i)re ly born   use d   j s et

j bye   f arepay airplay

j arm j   way v   last bye v aire

just   here is

that   just

torsion

Mont réal   wailing   inland kick pax

medusa wheat   devoid   pen t

pea t moss lock   than Denver rad io

shark talk   bellow vig   how e lug

king knot   dog crater   4xskids mm t   j

scope wine   rerun GR eek   street oxide

open shack D i o xon son ny   animism yook

to merlot   to Sookholme stand   [pls pls pls]

taskKafka shrubbery *vert*

tin ear Tom   goaway   fool Platt

bask marquee   Brochbank default   *vita skedaddle*

loose tooth

liz ar d love   Lisbon candle

liz beth ean dream candles   psychos is biz

cold em brace   progress pro fit

deck chair ana mnesis

per tink tink phoneme

per park walk   para dox talk

only back to   bookstore n un

ache sip   check shirt   you

tucked in   lost s ink   en gin e *purr*

lake silence

s tar moths   flying ant s   sun breaks

to get

to why

to absence work ing electro   change ch arges

to absen ce   car run   never chance page

to absenc e   e asy 4 0 ride   same warm p age

to oh   Debor ah   place of   why of time   ages

Sean G. Meggeson lives in Toronto, Canada, where he works as a psychoanalytic psychotherapist. He has written and lectured on such topics as Ricoeurian hermeneutics, neurodiversity, and interspecies intersubjectivity. He has published poetry and prose in a range of journals and magazines, including *Blaze Vox*, *Blood + Honey*, and *Die Leere Mitte*.

Statement: I like what Benjamin wrote in his essay, *Surrealism*: "In the world's structure dream loosens individuality like a bad tooth. This loosening of the self by intoxication is, at the same time, precisely the fruitful, living experience that allowed these people to step outside the domain of intoxication." I like using words to do this kind of thing that de-centers self, so I would say I relate to Benjamin's "these people."

David Wolf

from *More*

the river eels away
(from lunar elevation in vain as in name only
carried forth, idling eddies?)
in the sharp wash of the scythe

and a turn's hidden echo released inward,
vitally estranged—a rollicking endearment to please
the heckled envoy's lassoing spin

a whistle in the swirl of the water's curl—
a yucked-up frown raised on mussed laughter
under the nodding arch—reticence?

embellishment leans evasively—
voice shifts an attitude—titular innovation on it,
for sure somewhat noticeably

inveigh, inject some nourishment—
varnished and innovative to none,
to atonality's search impeding nestled space

not as memory's estate offs itself
in the nave or loo or like a yoyo's continuum
ascending roughly routed as in erosion's dunk

for once rather twice hence an immanence
dealt long I've noted gone error's dawn
dished in etched sheen

*

sharp churn, folds in the broad river—
    waters mussed in the shadow of the bell tower—
nests still nestled in the leaning trees
    routed in the lingering shine

*

the hulking boom of the great idea
the slick climb back up the spillway—
the flaw in the dirt to the filmic monk:
no thaw to vend
no weeping whim

you tout the crux and cube the lobe
the magi grow mum
dank just out of the vat
whizzing over the span in the smog
you miss the loon and pass on the root

all this shaken and weeded from the rug
the audience long-bodied as disorder
the summer wilt
the swab of time on a tilted pier
the ivied pram and the forked tomb

belief suspended and jiggling
in the gelatin of goodwill
hammers and expunges
dismisses the conclave's potions
snubs all resonance once held for rot

*

enough
effluvial new off with the ushering in
    of gleaming howls
nimbly expands nursed expanding the wasted
    outreach fluff or fur wild influx torn hellbent tug
    of hooping elaboration unsparing sweep
held entwined ringing till intercepted as such as needy
    as grown weary of it all not to say out to forage
in the blowsy grasses lots cast every aside a
    maxim of imploding nothingness
a grunt in the hoarfrost
of would-be lingering sap

the expectation to pander air once nurturing
now dense as sand

    more? yes I guess or just
    an attempt to live through
    it must should make the effort a tear
    in the fabric a forgotten fear
    under the table and so enough

namely then again to utter fumblingly so
mumbling thusly beaded a leeway of leaves yelling
wastrel-burrowed answers to satisfy
a tasteless interface an equinox of dispossession
ore's the pox upselling the trail's reach to each
achoo coursing holistically away

    *

toasted on the reruns tattered
and half-woozy in stellar garniture

a twig draws the oxen to its axis
its sway a tusk espied duped
over noted
torment heaving entitled
on what rung erring runes resting
upon a follow-up swansong
these attitudes tough to call epic rules
envious of the dunk
as not as done
hymned awry lute fussing wren oven-oval
zooming yuck it up
itchy noser
swag turfed elsewhere lush green and
lumbering in the shear assemblage a lull

the grime on the armchair
roughhousing like a new wave impressed
transversed to uphold
    redemption's emphases

noon in ruins avid gyre
the isle tunes in unto one rude egg

a sash for the meter

**

David Wolf is the author of seven collections of poetry, *Open Season, The Moment Forever, Sablier I, Sablier II, Visions* (with artist David Richmond), *Weir* (a micro-chapbook from Origami Poems Project), and *Seven.* His work has appeared in numerous literary magazines and journals, including *BlazeVOX, Cleaver Magazine, dadakuku, decomp, E·ratio, Exacting Clam, Indefinite Space, Lotus-eater Magazine, New York Quarterly, Otoliths, River Styx Magazine, Transom,* and *Utriculi.* He is a professor emeritus of English at Simpson College and serves as the poetry editor for *Janus Head: Journal of Interdisciplinary Studies in Literature, Continental Philosophy, Phenomenological Psychology, and the Arts.*

Artist's Statement:

These poems are from a long persona work in progress titled *More.* "More" is the surname of the speaker, whose poems foreground the music of language (a music sometimes melodic, sometimes dissonant) and a disjunctive approach to imagery.

Mark DuCharme

Sung as Guarded Motion

Things as ever often are
As air or error in the teeming digs
Curtained arrangement variously scuttled
Begun again as ever often hears
As revolting sometimes also seems resumed
To begin again as round as counted
Tune or tongue or heals precariously
Knotted in swivel with time bent cautiously
All imagined does does it say
In the wrong order temporally
Temporally up to date in kilter
Swoon relief a parting gift
Gorgeous as it does is ever
After gorge is all well wished
Seemingly seemingly apple mystique
Nightly menace boutique ample survival theater
Of bodies a multitude as ever being
Quiver incessant with night damage blooming

For instance, I was lurching
When I should have been yawning
For instance, I was yawning
When I should have been ministerial
A telegraph heap
A gated commune
Exit anywhere you never were
Sometimes, downtown is neither
A penny for your survival footage
Also, maybe junk solo folios
In plantform silliness
Out the window, beside a heap
Who made us unreflective
Why is truth the opposite of sky
Seen later, at a dead mirror

Stuffy, in its penmanship folly
Like true, repressive angels leaning
Whenever rhythm is the opposite of sun

Dreaming a Voice, I Wander Down to the Sea

You, who in great waters surge
Deeper than fear may go

Retune the caper of your violet joists
Have fears where summers soon may go

Once, I was an ape of puzzlement
The long year stretched before me like a crank

I seethed with a glimmer of the sun you hide in
I could make out no ingots 'til June

Would you know me, even as I did not know myself
Crazy, up to speed— with time apparently at a standstill

On the pier, where all gulls squawked
Contemplating the divers

Near the orchid pavilion, where I once took your picture
Petulant with croissants & mulberries

Skimpy tipper, concatenated warbler
Of thee, I am tipsy with perturbation

But if I tear up now, it's only to be bold
& Salve your blandishments with record-keeping

Don't hesitate to leverage
Muttered breath as a reproduction of smiles

Or append, by boatswain's speed
Those images that are brought forth

In a log heap, in the billiard room with flowers
Like a hole, sometimes, in the meaning of the sea

After the Hymns of the Birds

I'm not going to retype that lonesome word

Skies may be volatile

Knowledge is hearsay for the good

Toward what good do you aspire?

Though I still have my sunglasses on
I'll survive another day

When grief is my housekeeper
Tamarind usage won't quite be

*

Silence swarms the echo
It is a complex interchange
Built of bent lightning
By dreams' awful speed

The horizon bends
The time left
Construction is variable

Like plaster saints—
Impossible assets—
Thirst—
Carbon suffering

*

Things always decay
Go ask Johnny
If love is a room full of straw

An interior of broken phones
Until my socks point outward

The wind on my plate
Arrives— punctured

"The song hurts"— a quiet
Elsewhere— many here are pictured

With bamboo elements— description
Enhances the face

The song leans toward completion
An architect of vertiginous decay—

Like the hands of dead men
On the route no one can name

*

Where noon ruined yesterday
Like a penmanship thief

Erase the fear you're almost near
When elders play altos, to tell you goodbye

Them

1.
A taste of smoke settles
On the tongue
Children shout 'ladder, ladder' to no one
Everything takes five days

Of broken conference proposals
To remember to go on
Where the wicker's to be found
In quaint, antique storage rooms

The ones with more soda
Where we shouted out, 'thingamabob, thingamabob'
& Streets held fewer survivors—
How about you

Who bear a copy of lost realism
& Its sad numbers?
What fools! Go now & plunder
Whatever wickedness night steals

2.
Decide you won't yet be
With rancid filmstock
A complete list of household myths
Drawn on a map you'll never receive

Even if you eat at a glance
With fine reverb
Which, from birth, you might insist
The world cannot be

3.
Think, to install
Bright angels
As settled law
This is one way of flicking convenience on its head

Another is flung down like no one's raw
Oblique second industry
Or children whose faces (oboes)
Are too blue

As if their rhymes were the King's routing number
Its roots of night foretold
Banked on like carvings or
Last sentences

Coda:
Don't tell night
What the moon feels

Mark DuCharme's newest collection is *Thousands Blink Outside,* published in 2024 by C22 Open Editions. Other recent publications include *Here, Which Is Also a Place* from Unlikely Books; *Scorpion Letters* from Ethel; and his work of poet's theater, *We, the Monstrous: Script for an Unrealizable Film,* from The Operating System. His poetry has appeared widely in such venues as *BlazeVOX, Caliban Online, Colorado Review, Eratio, First Intensity, Gas, Indefinite Space, New American Writing, Noon, Offcourse, Otoliths, Shiny, Spinozablue, Talisman, Typo, Unlikely Stories, Utriculi, Word/ for Word, The Writing Disorder,* and *Poetics for the More-Than-Human World: An Anthology of Poetry and Commentary.* He lives in Boulder, Colorado, USA.

Heller Levinson

in as much as vexation wouldn't disappear, other

strategies were required.

   assimilate?   eradicate?   subordinate?

none of the above. the frosty

orange of the ineradicable diffuses,

perches, -- puckers.

a haunt peppers the formidable.

endless folds, relentless flurries.

another Sunday afternoon with swings

& sandcastles.

in as much as the masquerade

displaces, distorts, -- a

lopside on the shin of predictable

--

a loose, ascertaining, an

aroused kindling,

flagella foam

vacuole groom

-- *incur*,

relish

subterranean reveilles,

indecent,

probing,

stripped

in as much as maldoror

fumes, fustigates, … enfuries

        a smut on the
        lick of miasma

pestilential

leprous

     strangulating in vapor crunch, pistil

     clot, astringent debasement,

perilous

petrol

paucity

from Scurrilous Amber
abrade.

this is a love story.

without a love object.

Love without an object to plant that love is formless.

this is a formless love story.

p's & q's grow restless & disrespectful.

(Vermilion puckers,

bickers

(altruistic gestures

destabilize, there is

mayhem in Moscow

(contradiction fertilizes

fascination

(where in the aperture

is sore

formless is a renown void surfer

this is a love story bordering on home remedies

tralala   tralala

Δ   Δ

above board

through the looking glass

along came trolley

amitosis

atmosphere

anisometric

tabernacle

law abiding comfortable with airwaves rarely indecent measured in speech & bodily purport shortly came the dispatch which spun the whole caboodle out of control.

in as much as placement was paramount the role of measurement mushroomed.

the monopoly of metric valve spasms ultra lurch quake shiver

metric maldoror

'Calibration pollutes,' said the minister.

Heller Levinson's most recent books are *QUERY CABOODLE, SHIFT GRISTLE* (Black Widow Press, 2023), *THE ABYSSAL RECITATIONS* (Concrete Mist Press, 2024), *VALVULAR ASH* (BWP, 2024), Q*UERY CABOODLE 2* (Sulfur Editions, 2024), *Crossfall* (Sandy Press, 2024), with *CROSSFALL* (BWP) arriving summer 2025. His book, *LURE* (Black Widow Press, 2022), won the "2022 Big Other Poetry Book Award." Recent reviews:

https://sulfur-surrealist-jungle.com/2024/02/27/the-wild-poetics-of-questioning-in-heller-levinsons-work-by-mohsen-el-belasy/
https://sulfur-surrealist-jungle.com/2024/11/27/levinsons-quantum-foam-by-john-olson/?fbclid=IwZXh0bgNhZW0CMTAAAR3jusSInNUeL7l1Kf RbbgzgwTe9Dw-7z4Vx9E3erYGVsIzIPeJxB-DDccA_aem_DPGopB9pGDZdMhCmebZ9Pg

Daniel Barbiero

Magritte's Things

"In order for the objects which were revealed to us in childhood to continue to have the same power of revelation for us, they must be given new functions. So, for example, a link is created between a house and musical instrument, and a bilboquet is turned into a creature from a new mythology."

"I made paintings where the objects were represented with the appearance they have in reality, in a style sufficiently objective that the subversive effect...might exist again in the real world from which these objects had been borrowed...That pictorial experience which puts the real wold on trial, gives me a belief in the infinity of possibilities as yet unknown to life. I know I am not alone in affirming that their conquest is the sole aim and the sole valid reason for the existence of man."

With these words – the first from a 1946 statement on titles, the second from the 1938 autobiography/artist statement "Lifeline" – Magritte expresses not only an artistic first principle but a poetics of things generally. Things must have their poetry – what Magritte calls their power of revelation – restored to them through an art whose subversive effect would carry over into the real world in which these things are. How to do that was the basic problem his art set out to solve. As he hints above, the solution would consist in alienating things from their everyday functions, or modes of being, and reimagining what they are, or what they could be, through a method of association. What Magritte is proposing, in other words, is a poetics of things in which our ontological relation to things – our relating to things as the beings they are, on the basis of that which makes them the kind of beings they are – is transposed from a mundane to an imaginative plane. Under this poetic dispensation our ontological relation to things would no longer consist in grasping them as pieces of equipment, decorative objects, or the furniture of daily life more generally, but as catalysts suggesting meanings through the imaginative activation in us of more or less elaborate webs of association, affect, and affinity.

The Analogical Image

What Magritte wished to do was to transform his things from mundane physical objects into complex figures generating meaning not on the basis of what we ordinarily know of them, or think we know of them, but on the basis a particular kind of defamiliarization. It was a defamiliarization grounded in analogy. The links Magritte refers to above aren't links forged on the basis of readily available likenesses between things – likenesses of function, or appearance or other qualities. For how is a house functionally like a musical instrument, or a baluster like a mythological creature? Instead, they are links that work through analogies that work in two ways: first, between things which are brought together precisely because they are in some way unlike, and second, between things which are linked by an affinity, but one that had to be "discovered." Magritte described both approaches in his 1938 autobiography/artist statement "Lifeline":

"One night in 1936, I awoke in a room where a cage and the bird sleeping in it had been placed. A magnificent error caused me to see an egg in the cage instead of the bird. I then grasped a new and astonishing poetic secret, because the shock I experienced had been provoked precisely by the affinity of the two objects, the cage and the egg, *whereas previously I used to provoke this shock by bringing together objects that were unrelated.* Ever after that revelation I sought to discover if objects other than the cage could not likewise manifest – by bringing to light some element peculiar to them and rigorously predetermined – the same evident poetry that the conjunction of the egg and the cage had succeeded in producing." (Gablik, p. 183. Emphasis in the original.)

In either case – of analogy by dissimilarity or of analogy by hidden affinity – Magritte's painterly poetic was consistent with the Surrealist idea of the image. The idea was originally expressed in Pierre Reverdy's 1918 statement in *Nord-Sud* and was subsequently elaborated by André Breton in a number of theoretical writings. Because it is foundational to the Surrealist theory of the image, and to Magritte's method of portraying things as well, it's worth quoting:

"The image is a pure creation of the mind.

It cannot be born from a comparison but from a juxtaposition of two more or less distant realities.

The more the relationship between the two juxtaposed realities is distant and true, the stronger the image will be – the greater its emotional power and poetic reality…" (quoted in *Manifestoes*, p. 20.)

The image is the product of thought – and recall here Magritte's claim that his painting was the "visible description of thought" (Danchev, p. xxxiv) – which, through other than logical means, joins objects, ideas, or images from ontological domains more or less removed from each other into poetic images that carry an affective charge.

André Breton further developed the idea of the Surrealist image into a theory of Surrealist analogy in his 1947 essay "Ascendant Sign". There, he asserted that

"For me the only *manifest truth* in the world is governed by the spontaneous, clairvoyant, insolent connection established under certain conditions between two things whose conjunction would not be permitted by common sense...Poetic analogy...transgresses the rules of deduction to let the mind apprehend the interdependence of two objects of thought located on different planes. Logical thinking is incapable of establishing such a connection…" (*Free Rein*, pp. 104-105. Emphasis in the original.)

With the idea of Surrealist analogy, we have the basic framework for grasping what Magritte was trying to do with his things.

Things and Scenarios

If the new functions Magritte gave his objects were based on analogical correspondences rather than utilitarian value, how did he pull it off as a practical matter? By positioning his objects within extraordinary scenarios hinting at an alogical narrative of some sort. Magritte's is a markedly literary kind of painting.

The idea of arranging things in combinations that defy everyday logic was an inheritance from de Chirico. Magritte esteemed de Chirico's painting from the time he first encountered it, which appears to have been in late 1923, when he saw *Le Chant d'amour* (*The Song of Love*) reproduced in a publication (Danchev, p. 110). Some of his early paintings, like 1926's *La Traversée difficile* (*The Difficult Crossing*) and 1927's *La Statue volante* (*The Flying Statue*), borrow some of de Chirico's compositional forms and allude to his vocabulary of objects. But Magritte went beyond that to create scenarios of his own, involving

"The creation of new objects, the transformation of known objects, the change of material for certain objects, the use of words combined with images, the putting to work of ideas offered by friends, the utilization of certain visions from half-sleep or dreams..." (Gablik, p. 183)

Thus it isn't the deliberately dull, realistic portrayal of the thing that undermines its mundane meaning and makes for the volatility of the image. Instead, it's the overall scenario that produces the volatile image through its staging of an analogy. A green apple is unlike a face until a face is concealed behind an unnaturally large green apple in *Le Fils de l'homme* (*The Son of Man*); a rose is unlike a dagger until, through their secret affinity, a dagger is made to grow from its stem in *Le Coup au coeur* (*The Blow to the Heart*); an umbrella and a glass are functionally opposed to each other – one is used to repel water and the other to collect and hold it – until they are analogized by their common relationship to water in *Les Vacances de Hegel* (*Hegel's Holiday*).

The juxtaposition of unrelated or secretly related things; the self-subversion of things whose apparent properties don't properly belong to them; the thing mislabeled with the name of another thing – all of these scenarios introduce into the thing an analogical tension built on a contradiction between our everyday expectations and the recalcitrant evidence on the canvas. These things just won't behave the way things are supposed to behave. The scenario, in short, is an event consisting of the defiance of the mundane. In defying the mundane meaning of things, Magritte's scenarios perform an ontological sleight of hand through which that on the basis of which we recognize things as the things they are is distorted and thus undermined. For Magritte, the ontological destabilization of things, and the attribution to them of hidden analogical meanings, was a way of making the world subjective. Or better, of reminding us that the world had always been subjective. As he expressed this quasi-Kantian view in "Lifeline," "...we see the world as being outside ourselves even though it is only a mental representation of it that we experience inside ourselves" (Gablik, p. 184).

Things and Words

Arguably the most effect scenarios Magritte set up in reimagining his things were those in which words were paired with images. Beginning in 1927, Magritte produced a series of paintings titled *Le Cle des songes* (*The Interpretation of Dreams*) in which a series of images of objects were mislabeled with the names of apparently unrelated objects – with the exception of the last image in the series, which was labeled with the correct name. What Magritte was trying to show with this series is summed up in the following comments made by his friend Paul Nougé in 1936:

"We are...faced with an obvious truth: the word can never do justice to the object; it is foreign to it as if indifferent.

But the unknown name may also hurl us into a world of ideas and images, leading us to a mysterious point on the mental horizon, where we encounter things wondrous and strange..." (Danchev, p. 166)

There are a couple of points here. The first is the observation that the relationship between an object and the word that designates it is arbitrary and not based on any inherent affinity between the word and the thing. It's an observation that in the West goes back at least to Plato's *Cratylus*. The second, more original point, is that the encounter of the object-picture and the name that doesn't fit it somehow makes for a "wondrous and strange" meaning – creates, in effect, a Surrealist image through a hidden analogy. Before looking at this second point, a brief comment on how the word "can never do justice to the object."

As the sign of a concept, the word, and particularly the noun designating a material thing in the world, takes us away from the thing as a physical object and gives us instead the thing as Idea and representation. The thing is converted from token to Type, from contingent existent to Ideal – in short, from *that* to *what*. In the process, we go from the visible to the invisible, which we might see as a form of compromise or alienation. We no longer relate to the thing as a thing, but as the (imperfect) representative of an Idea.

This form of alienation isn't restricted to the word, though. An image of a thing can alienate it as well, and in the same way. The image of the thing, as opposed to the word naming it, has an ambiguity built into it. It can be read as representing the thing in its imperfect physical embodiment – as the visual presentation of an aspect of the thing, as we would see it in the world -- or as the non-discursive representation of the Idea or essence of the thing, as Plotinus asserted of the wall carvings in Egyptian temples. Because he favored a flat, illustrational style, Magritte in many of his paintings played on this ambiguity, whether intentionally or not. For example, I have argued elsewhere that for reasons having to do not only with stylistic considerations but with overall compositional logic as well, Magritte's depiction of the pipe labeled "this is not a pipe" may be read in this second manner. But this is an exception. For the most part, Magritte seems to have intended his object-images to be taken at face value, which is to say at the level of their appearance rather than as allusions to abstract concepts. This is why, for example, in a letter of 26 April 1964 he gently upbraided a curator who labeled some of his images as "symbols" and asserted instead that they "are objects...and not symbols...My conception of painting...tends to restore to objects their value as objects..." (Quoted in Danchev, p. 37). In the *Le Cle des songes* series the pairing of the image of the thing with the name of another thing resolves the potential ambiguity of the image in favor of its function as representing the thing in the world rather than the thing as concept or Ideal. In order for the series to work – in order for the catalytic effect of its word and image pairings to emerge – we must read the image of the thing as the thing it depicts. When we read the image as the thing and not as a conceptual substitute for the thing, we maintain the ontological gap between the image and the word and prevent it from collapsing into a heap of abstraction.

If, by being reduced (or being elevated – there is a choice in how we look at it) to a concept or Ideal the thing is compromised and alienated by the word that (correctly) designates it, it is alienated to a further degree when mislabeled by the word for another, explicitly opposed, thing. The mismatch between the image of the thing, which points us in one direction, and the name of another thing, which points us in an entirely different direction, accomplishes an ontological displacement that makes the thing conspicuous by compelling us, in the context of looking at a work of visual art, to stop and focus our attention on the reality of the thing, through its image, in order to determine what exactly it's supposed to be, given its pairing with the name of something else. The mismatched word makes the thing *qua* thing conspicuous in a way that it ordinarily wouldn't be and renders it out of place: it is made strange, *atopos*. It becomes the uncomfortable object of a too-close scrutiny. By breaking the conventional relationship between word and thing in this drastic manner, Magritte displaces the thing from its place within the normal order of things and creates a tension between the verbal and visual meanings that potentially, at least, catalyzes a supervening poetic meaning. Which may become its "true" meaning.

This brings us back to Breton's idea of the analogy based on unlikely affinity. It's possible to find linkages between the words and the images they mislabel through missing third terms. For example, here is poet Mark Young's response, in *The Magritte Poems*, to the first painting in the *Le Cle des songes* series. Here Magritte depicts a briefcase with the word for sky underneath it; a pocketknife labeled "bird" ("*l'oiseau*"); a leaf tagged as a table; and a sponge, curiously enough, properly named as a sponge. Young's response to the painting sees a

> ...confusion
> when something is
> given an entirely different
> name to that we
> usually ascribe to it. Is the
> briefcase labelled sky
> to be our travelling
> companion or the cover
> under which we
> set out on what
> began a journey
> & is now a vestibule?

The confusion fostered by Magritte's misnaming potentially resolves itself in the hidden analogies an imaginative viewer might find in the painting's contradictory word/image pairings. Young brings together the briefcase and the sky by positing a likeness deriving from their complementary functions in the context of travel: to accompany us on the trip, and to provide the natural ceiling under which we move, respectively. The idea of travel is the hidden third term that mediates these two images and supplies their affinity for each other. But as Young's poem demonstrates, it's a third term that has to be divined; it requires an act of creative will in the form of hypothetical interpretation. Creative interpretation turns out to be indispensable to the "subversive effect" Magritte wished his work to have.

It was Magritte's overall intention that his paintings impel viewers to refound their relationships to the things in their worlds – that through their own processes of inference, association, and metaphorical linkages, viewers would begin to see ontological analogies they'd never seen before. And in doing so, would "put[] the real world on trial" and give rise to "an infinity of possibilities as yet unknown to life."

References:

André Breton, *Manifestoes of Surrealism*, tr. Richard Seaver and Helen R. Lane (Ann Arbor: U of Michigan Press, 1972). Internal cite to *Manifestoes*.

_____, "Ascendant Sign," in *Free Rein*, tr. Michel Parmentier and Jacqueline D'Amboise (Lincoln, NE: U of Nebraska Press, 1995). Internal cite to *Free Rein*.

Alex Danchev with Sara Whitfield, *Magritte: A Life* (New York: Pantheon, 2020). Internal cites to Danchev.

Suzy Gablik, *Magritte* (Boston: New York Graphic Society/Little Brown & Co., 1976). Internal cites to Gablik.

Mark Young, *The Magritte Poems* (Santa Barbara, CA: Sandy Press, 2024).

Daniel Barbiero is a writer, double bassist, and composer in the Washington DC area. He writes about the art, music, and literature of the classic avant-gardes of the 20th century as well as on contemporary work; his essays and reviews have appeared in *Arteidolia, The Amsterdam Review, Heavy Feather Review, periodicities, Word for/Word, Otoliths, Offcourse, Utriculi, London Grip,* and elsewhere. He is the author of *As Within, So Without,* a collection of essays published by Arteidolia Press; his score *Boundary Conditions III* appears in *A Year of Deep Listening* (Terra Nova Press).

Website: https://danielbarbiero.wordpress.com.

Alan Catlin

Swallow Dazzled By the Glare of Red Pupil

Eye
Eye without
Eye without lashes
    without
Eye
      lashed to the sky
        cantankerous
bird in flight

hides
hides in
hides in a
      prism
      a prison of fractured light

The red circle
    red dwarf
    red ball
      glared
      glares
      glaring
        splendor

Woman with Birds in Front of the Sun

The sun a death mask
    leaking harlequin tears

    scratching as claws
    leaving long unhealing

wounds on sky

The watching woman's eyes
    solar spots
    her fingers

        nascent fires

for birds
to perch on

Alan Catlin has many chapbooks and full-length collection in poetry and prose. He has written in many different styles and forms from straight narrative poems, to nearkus (like haikus but not quite) to unclassifiable experimental poetry that can be found in his collections *Memories* (Alien Buddha) and *Memoires Too* (Dos Madres). Selections from these books and the long work in progress, *Ongoing Memoires*, were published in *Otoliths* and *Synchronized Chaos*. He is the poetry and reviews editor of misfitmagazine.net

Statement of purpose, These poems are inspired by Klee, these poems and are a scattering of language, words in space that connect somewhere in our inner being as all poetry and art does.

John Bradley

The Secretary of Defense Accidentally Texts the Ballad of the Five Babbling Grackles

What am I to do
  with five gabbling grackles in my hand.

One says, *Beware the sleek beak*
  glinting with wet light.

One says, *X = the moon*
  before it was the moon.

Another says, *Never talk dirty*
  near a bee hive.

One strongly advises, *Sterilize the participles*
  afloat in the Potomac.

One says, *Silent anthills on the tongue*
  carry no weight.

What can be done
  with five babbling grackles in the hand.

Why My Arm Might Give You the Roman Salute
For Elon Musk

Whenever I see the sky, cloudy or bare naked, I just can't
help it. My right arm performs the Roman salute.

Every time I see a child making a monkey face, I tell my arm,

Now stay cool, friend. Don't weird the kid out. And then
my arm goes up, and just like that, I give that little citizen

a stunning Roman salute. Who invented it? My right arm

tells me about a soldier who hated Julius Caesar, after
Caesar slept with the soldier's wife, and his sister, and

his mother, and both his grandmothers. And his dog.

One day Caesar nods to the crowd, and the soldier's arm
goes up. The first known Roman salute. All I know

is that when I see cars collide, and hear sirens, and see

paramedics with moony faces, and everyone looks like the air
was let out of them, I just want the world to evaporate,

and so does my arm. Then it happens. My arm gets rigid

and goes up. Sure, I get some dirty looks, but, hey,
it's no big thing, really. I mean the Romans were pretty

smart, and I don't mind telling you, so is my right arm.

Thereupon I Kept Falling Out of My Eyes: An Interview with Pere Ubu

Q. Where do we go when all the words run out?
A. It's a war that never should have happened.

Q. Where do the words go, when they go? And do we follow?
A. Eggs, eggs, eggs.

Q. In that moment when every word has dissolved, where do we
go?
A. That's not gonna happen. We're not gonna let that happen. But
you're not being very nice.

Q. Will we still be here when all the words leave us?
A. I'm not saying good, bad, or indifferent.

Q. What happens. To you, to me. When words are no more?
A. I don't have a hundred percent confidence in anything, okay? I don't have a hundred percent confidence that we're gonna finish this interview.

Q. Words. Gone. Vamoosed. And then?
A. You don't know that.

Q. Words, they slip away, abandon us. What do we do?
A. I probably wouldn't be inclined to tell you. I mean, you're being dishonest.

Q. All the words, even these words, disappear. What happens then?
A. I don't trust a lot of people. I don't trust you.

Q. And so, the words shall go, and we shall go thence too?
A. Rapidity and speed and other things.

Q. Words we wooed, spooned, tongued. Once they leave, left?
A. I want to leave that as a big, fat secret.

Q. When the words return to dust, to dust do we return?
A. Eggs, eggs, eggs.

All the Tired Starlight Gathering in Your Inexhaustible Eye (Or How to Write a Title for Your Immortal Poem)

1. Isn't *All* rather a bit much? Maybe *Some* or *A Lot* or, if you must, *Crowds*. Overstatement makes you sound less trustworthy. You would be wise to let demagogues and drone operators continue to woo *All*.

2. Why *Tired*? Why not *Tiered*? Or *Timed*? Even better: *Unspooling, Coagulating, Itching, Shifting, Shouting*. How can a poem tells us that starlight will tire? No one wants to hear that. You are the one who sounds exhausted.

3. OK, *Starlight* is heavenly, stellar, cosmic, but not kicky. Go for the underused and underpraised: *Hairlight, Mushroomlight, Broomlight*. If you were forced to eat a bowl of *Starlight*, you would never want to see that word again. Turn away from the stars and look around and down.

4. Everybody wants to *Gather*, but not inside a poem. Have you ever seen a line around the block to peer inside a poem? Maybe there would be a line to see a criminal thrown into a poem for a life sentence. I'd pay to see a poet have to live inside their own poem for just 30 days.

5. Must the poem belong to a boring *Your*? Why not the *Coronor's*? Or the *Photographer's*? We don't care about this anonymous *Your*, which could be you, or maybe the reader, or maybe someone's uncle standing behind me right now, yawning, staring at a fly on the sky.

5. What is *Inexhaustible*, besides the ambition of a poet? Maybe Buster Keaton running from a house on wheels that wants to mate with him and birth a herd of tiny houses on tiny wheels. Go for *Inevitable, Invisible, Indigestible*. Even *Instantaneous*. Make us weep in wonder.

7. Finally, we visit the *Eye* that never sleeps or wakes. The *Eye* that is a god watching all we say or do. We've all inherited that from Kafka. Let the *Eye* become an *Ocean* with many legs. Too many legs. Let this Ocean stalk us. And watch us try to run.

Spring Air for Lute and Dulcimer

Oh, let the hungry squirrel gnosh
upon the tender red buds
of the maple, you say,
so many buds there are.

    As if you were the lord

of earth and arbor, permitting
a grubby peasant to pilfer
a moldy potato or two.

But should a crow,
swollen with anger
one moonless midnight, enter
your bedchamber,

How quickly
your hand would reach
beneath the bed, fumble
for the baseball bat,

The hard wood ready
to strike whatever sparks
sweet fear
in the brain's deep taproot.

John Bradley has appeared in *Caliban, Cloudbank, DMQ Review, Hotel Amerika, Lake Effect, Otoliths, SurVision,* and other journals. My most recent book is *As Blood Is the Fruit of the Heart: A Book of Spells* (Dos Madres Press). A frequent reviewer for *Rain Taxi,* I am currently a poetry editor for *Cider Press Review.*

Recent social and political events have been sparking my poetry of late, as you can see. I've been deeply influenced by surrealist poets such as Vallejo, Lorca, and Tomaz Salamun, the way their poems probe and reveal the subconscious.

John Grey

NEWS FROM NOWHERE

Lost arrows have come home to roost.
The no-name river runs shoeless.
In this year's fashions,
most women dress with the wounded in mind.
The Lincoln Memorial is outlined with razor blades.
A gay man was found living in his own roof gutter.
For the least among us,
a fried-chicken takeout place
is the first thing they see
when they open their eyes in the morning.
The world's scientists look good in their invisible faces.
We're living in the dawn of the age of authority figures.
This coming year, three mountains will be replaced by flags.
The food chain has been shrunk and is now a mere bracelet.
Ear wax is the new acne.
Lit candles cry tears.
The window for finding true love is a victim of double glazing.
Life-and-death struggles are now a float
in Macy's Thanksgiving Day parade.
There is no sports news worth thinking about.
If you insist, your team lost and your star player
was impaled on a spear.
Religion is now classified as a martial art.
The Rolling Stones have nothing left to give.
Your inner life can no longer make it up the stairs.
Where there's life, there are failed prophecies of the apocalypse.
New discoveries are no one's fault.
That sound you hear is your car's license plate
begging for forgiveness.
A diving board was found suspiciously wrapped.
It is now legal to marry a flying kite.
A small, land-bordered African country
is the first to be recognized as a Reality TV nation.

There are no free lunches but you can still get snake-bit for
nothing.
The weather's been overheard complaining about people.
This just in: your best buddy won't be there for you.
Praying for your opponent's death is now the favored
political strategy for office-seekers.
Stay tuned for the news from somewhere
which will follow this news from nowhere bulletin.
As an aside, talking heads are now being returned to their rightful
necks.

STARDUST

In the fountain at night,
it sparkled.
My hand rippled the waters
but none of it came off on me.
It was my flesh,
its gleam
and the cool liquid.
Everything else was stone.
This was just one more
confluence of things,
where I spend time alone.
The stone was solid,
like the earth itself.
The water was soft
and easy to the touch.
Other than my eyes,
my hand is the part of me
that can work best
in any setting.
It was gentle
and curious
on this occasion.
But, of all,
the stardust was my favorite.
It drew all of my attention

and it wasn't even there.
It wasn't an epiphany
Nor a revelation.
Merely an incentive.
Find it.
Spend time with it.
Then go seek it elsewhere.

SOMEONE DROWNED

Cops jostle and shove the riverbank crowd.
Rescue drag the dripping boy from the current,
wrap him in a sheet,
whisk him away.

The sheriff takes a moment to hate his job.
The sun's setting.
The light's fading.

The river is sluggish here,
has no interest in getting to the gulf before its time.
And it's silver and shallow,
seemingly as harmless as a wading pool.

Yet, mild-mannered as it may be,
it's still a killer.
This boy is not the first.

The mob dissipates.
The ambulance screams into the distance.
People come in ones and twos now,
to stare at the surface,
to imagine whatever floats on down as another child.
They don't speak, afraid it could be their own.

Then a car screeches.
The river's silver glint succumbs to shadow.
It's cool and dark.

A few kids hang outside the old abandoned opera house.
The current communes with the dock,

sounds calmer than it's ever been.

Tragedy dissolves, leaving everything normal.
No more blank eyes.
The motel neon sees to that.
No more lifeless flesh.
Not now that the bars are hopping.

BLATANCY

A stone repeated again, dead, all the windows
having their say, cruel heat from the base of the sun,
bad enough the birds all want to blow the last of the
cool air then I carried you there you are to a time
when I to rail, tugboat's

        Until the anniversary
we had nutmeg-
when   you were still alive,
will be   the inverse
will die   down
Wind   unlashes the
with the   same velocity —
world is fine   and then
You carried me, your
daughter, your death— your
new stone away

into each other's mouths.
Now I know where the breath of life has fled.

But every day in this year, memory
makes a come-back.
come back.

grip the ti   les. And
guests are put o   ut.
          guests   could barely
guests say, half foot of
sand, hands raised like
he caresses the hollow
blare, huddle in benches I
would blow I would
blow the

          rod dropped sea
and bar

John Grey is an Australian poet, US resident, recently published in *New World Writing, River And South* and *The Alembic*. Latest books, "Subject Matters"," Between Two Fires" and "Covert" are available through Amazon. Work upcoming in *Paterson Literary Review, White Wall Review* and *Cantos*.

Dominik Slusarczyk

The Mountain

Know nothing matters.
Try anyway.
Die anyway.

Dust

I love dust and
You love dust but
We hate each other like
Cats hate bath time.

Anvil Air

I used to want air:
I wanted it sinking in
My luxury lungs,
Stroking my fair forehead,
Right underneath my falling form.
All my life I wanted air.
I never knew it
Was so bitter.
I never knew it was what
Killed my first babysitter.

The Pretty Deer

Can you see the pretty deer?
Some of them have spikes on their heads.
I wonder if they
Know we love them.
I wonder if they
Know some people want them dead.

Relapse

Knowledge is nice but
Ignorance is easier.

Dominik Slusarczyk is an artist who makes everything from music to painting. He was educated at The University of Nottingham where he got a degree in biochemistry. His poetry has been published in various literary magazines including *California Quarterly* and *Taj Mahal Review*. His poetry was nominated for Best of the Net by *New Pop Lit,* and was a finalist in a couple of competitions. His full-length poetry collection *Reaction* is out now with *Cyberwit.*

Heath Brougher

It's the End of the World as We Know It {And I Feel Jived}

Laboratory grapes create unpsychedelic states
sponsored by your limestone lies as you
lick up your oligarchic key lime pie.

Memories erased the taste
of sweetened freest days outplayed
soured by overconfident sighs.

Red and white and blue are bled
when musky trumpets sing forth the lead
embracing bleached out heads.

Pork pie hats are hung beside the tree on every rung
as we burn thorough a pangful noose.

Menticidal freaks will stalk the poets and the priests
so they can raise their Kakistocracy
and vaporize democracy
when automatic wokeness reigns———>
values turn to tokened screens
puking pixelated vomiting
as you eat your blue light cake
to further hollow out the holes within the souls
of a country that could've been eating steak.

The Usual

elusive quarry

a twisted knife

the body

of battered

Joseph K

and

I.

Wrongplace Wrongtime

The Confuscious Dream Satellites are machines that produce
emptiness—they forge phoniness—they push forth the rampant
poisonous mirrorism of a society gimped and limped amucken.
Every theater is tantamount to being back in Plato's cave where
they sit and watch the fools they've elevated into rich role models
make further foals of themselves; only it's worse than Plato's cave
because the people know what they see isn't real and there is a way
out of their mental servitude but few dare ever wander into the
daylight; they prop up, propel, pallidly promote and perpetuate
hatred and division through the propaganda films they show on
loop; mindlessly taking orders from Napoleon and Big Brother and
Caligula.

They crush dissent, erase history—leaving a numb void in their
wake.

The Gist of Kakistocracy

The school principal inquired as to why the boy was sent to
detention and was beyond nonplussed when the teacher spake thus:
"He keeps talking about something called 'freedom.' Even says he
'has' it—whatever the fuck that means! He's obviously whacked
out of his mind on some kind of drug and I do not want him my

classroom. Suspend him. Bleed him. Gut him. Do your fuckin'
thing, man!"

Al's Attempt at Reading My Horrendous Handwriting

- "28"
- "[unintelligible or crossed out text]"
- "Blue Train"
- "
- "Gulls are f..!" [The rest is obscured or indistinct.]
- "|[..] all [perhaps 'hope'] all well [.]"
- [Further illegible or partially obscured lines]
- "I..?] took out for walk"
- ...perhaps 'shipboard' or something similar] on board the Sierra."
- "f..? nicely settle[...] to into the train"

Ode to Amis

It seems with each new year
we have finally arrived at the one meant
to be called the Year of Behaving Strangely—
only to realize how wrong we were
when December dies into a winter
of another disappeared year
as we realize the year should've been known
as the Year of the Planecrash
or the Year of the Nuclear Bomb.

Heath Brougher is editor-in-chief of Concrete Mist Press. His
most recent publication is "Beware the Bourgeois Doomsday
Fantasy" (Sandy Press, 2024).

karl kempton

angle of shadow & length
the horizon's lift & bow
set trajectory wrongly assigned
to old man sol we round

at end of axis swing days & middle days
shadows descending or climbing
chumash measured in ritual

others performed too but unlooked for
except serpent of light slithering
kukulcán pyramid at chichén itzá

beach & dunes walked here
belong not to north america

as crow flies ends 55 miles east of my keyboard san andreas fault

this the pacific plate
northwest 3 to 4 inches a year

we ride farallon plate scuff remains
heaped on monterey micoplate

anxious to unchain
as archipelago chain

channel islands south
elbowed 90 degrees

offshore pioneers
on arguello microplate

microplates' boundary fault
runs arguello canyon

channels persistent upwelling
feeding lush eco systems

in the bite 1969 oil spill
earth day's amniotic fluid

parties won't stop the slide
to inevitable uncivilized collapse

tectonics rubbed cliff
walls smooth glisten

chumash rock art
vibrate every rocket launch

mankind not commanded
to dominate nature in genesis

within nature manage
own self be human

damage nearly complete
from mistranslation & karma

each morning upon waking
we step into clothes day furnishes

light provides attributes of weave
& weft upon destined to walk out
the door into greetings from love

walk not self encumbered
with assumption unguided

each day a letter of love sent
to a page for your book of life

if unable to read learn script
of intuition for geography of
canyon full of attachments

turned upside down before you
the pinnacle of transcendence

reflecting

downslope
north
as
i
walked
the
fallow
soil

&
reflected
on
sun
reflection

off
cars
parked
a
mile
south
behind
me

chemically
tainted
strawberry
field
harvest

as
i
walked

the
chemical
free

farm
work
road
to
the
stand

walking
the
farmer's
dream
to
nourish
his
community

under
foot

back
in
time

another
farmer
dreamt

his
map
of
this
field

rows

as
if
unfolded

old
dollar
bills

chemically
fed
&
sprayed

mono
crop
strawberries

from
agriculture
industrial
flooring

when
plowed

or
sprayed
blown
by

breeze
or
wind

or
conveyed
under
the
roof
of
inversion

chemicals
&
chemically
laced
dust

into
neighborhoods

21
induced
symptoms

quarter
mile
radius

gone
in
3
months

when
stopped

the
ag
commissioner
turned
his
back
&
and
walked

away

a
mile

in
fact
behind
me

workers'
chemically
laced
cloths

removed
at
home

sprays
&
dust
drift
east
up
the
escarpment

into
mesa
homes

here

we
fought
many
years

sweeter
&
richer
the

food
by
the
year

shade rolls up slides window
blinding light bathes an innocent youth

opened to mysteries of vistas unknown
how again to bliss bathe in unconditional love

amazed in a maze not knowing in a maze
born into church lit by hell fire & brimstone

proving its lies divine offers a taste
of the real becomes a journey compass

through chaff covered traditions
identical undefinable core at heart

of matters that matter all on the line
| stroke of the one walked radius awake

to circle's center on circumference
knowing or not all on line up for grabs

yet hand passes through how many
miss the pointless point eras old

karl kempton (https://www.karlkempton.net/) lives with his beloved wife, Ruth, in Oceano, California. His works are widely published nationally and internationally in anthologies and in over 60 titles including *selected lexical & visual mathematical poetry 1976-2022* by Cold River Press. Awarded the Environmental Stewardship Award, 2024, by The Northern Chumash Tribal Council for his "advocacy for the Oceano Dunes and the Chumash Heritage National Marine Sanctuary as an esteemed colleague and supporter for the environment."

Julia Rose Lewis

watertight

it is only a pewter moon
antimony open
for the bed is the world turned door upside water
intertidally is dillydally lay me down snail
a shell will find my foot
tooth
itself fair play for the love of oval lives
also known as an airplane flying over a great lake
fluorescent light to canter
dear wash a shore
could be beating a dead horse could be cumulonimbus

a body lying down is missing cumulonimbus
if only fulfilling a lime moon
ashes to wash a shore
open to rainwater
canter
winter is a gray house with gray trim and a blue door
also known as a great lake
is fair play for a snail
all the ways in which a shell lives
is given in gastropubs and the small publishers fair to foot
salt tooth

to goat tooth
they beach themselves before the cumulonimbus
sends more sand to cover one foot
falls on a linen moon
circle circle intersection will give a moss egg oval lives
a rolling wash a shore
is also known as a terrestrial snail
operculum open
lake
and cold water canter
sore seriously is a wooden door

it is a holding in hand kind of door
water tooth
and inward spiral lends distance to canter
kicking up clodhopper pearls the cumulonimbus
sends an anvil lake
it takes a fountain turned upside down before a foot
is an artificial fall into the open
imagine the clouded could landing on the moon
is fear play for snail
lives
ashes to ashes wash a shore

shell to wash a shore
we all fall downtown ring around a door
bell is little obsolete lives
steamboat tooth
then barnstable also known as the new snail
toward the clouded could from the rocking horse canter
ringing a ring around the waning moon
cumulonimbus
is overwhelming home memories open
fair play for molochnyi lyman estuary or lake
or foot water

impossible blue mirrors the sound turned upside down and a foot
I am sorry wash a shore
for calling a like a lake
in the obsolete sense tilted about a bird door
to flirt with the airplane in the open
water lives
can one love a person as one would love a cumulonimbus
with with interest is only a tooth
moon
now waning is also known as a snail
making a canter

it is a clockwork canter
ring around the wound to bind the foot
truth then is string wound in a ball and tied to a snail

wash a shore
for the love of the littorinimorpha moon
necklace days begin to make bodies equal lake water
rabbit tooth
then is only a pellucid door
do what you ought to add the acid to the cumulonimbus
sinking an absolute border hole to open
also known as shell lives

to be level with the falling leaves then lives
inside the cold weather canter
phone open
nightmare also known as here eye the left foot
trotting out this trauma makes a cumulonimbus
snail
leaves a trail all the way to the sanded door
wash a shore: can one love a person as one would love the water
fraught tooth
then the freight boat beneath a booming moon
is the body of a giant white rabbit reflected in the lake

a fish with white flesh found in the whole lake
the great auk lives
in this water braying is fair play for a penguin moon
to say again can one love a necklace as one would love a canter
a circle of light about a tooth
then yellow eyebrow or supercilium on the open
mind then a rockhopper turns on a wash a shore
foot
turned outside door
recalls oval versus anvil cumulonimbus
sending hail and snow falling as a snail?

snail water
for the love of heavy rain replicates the lake
electric cumulonimbus
able to take inside wind headed lives
door

industry is trying to see the super moon
and the clouded could foot
fraught is its own past participle like canter
it is centering a wash a shore
to be holding power also known as obsolete tooth
there was yesterday and the day open

open
now where the pattern for the love of honey is trailing a snail
little tooth
truth then is fear play for the lake
wish wash a shore
all the ways a cumulonimbus will sow water
a narrow arena to canter
running around the point our whole lives
inside the galley the goat umbrellas and the foot
turning white is a wind headed door
the cold clay dust standing under a clam moon

the cumulonimbus is cold hosing the pain open
to canter is a horse is trial learning for a snail
lives apologetic tooth
if footfall is locating where to wind the yarn around the lake
I remember the wooden door also known as wash a shore
it is only an ointment moon on the wound following water

rabbit boy

rabbit rabbit in the wall
is only longing red light to save glow and glare
a pair of baby rabbits growing under his eyes
say back away man
a main to waste away to wither there
red is absent the opposite rabbit
it is waves bending around the earth then
a deep eclipse red is afraid
it is calling on electromagnetic radiation
it is moaning like a fortified town laying down in the wood

in the night not quite barnstable black
call back a hematology moon
night vision is trying trouble blinking
eye pry preserving visual capabilities in low light conditions
he is special red and infrared and fraught and eye afraid

unentitled

a line in the nightmare
that free will learned
and a rabbit did not is that
idea will paint forget me nots naturally
and not little blue stars fired
in the sense night life found wood
metal whale tooth then
a flat elongated form for stirring
and laying down ointments
eye mean
the cauline leaf is blue green
grazing the horse rabbit beside tulips
and inside the silicone tulips
beside the silicone spatula in vases saying
the line is lengthening even in the history of spit
then the spat is alright to say eye spy
spittle flying over the flowers
wood and silicone and edible bubbles
in blue and green and gray hues saying
the wrist flickers into flowering the idea
of hitting the fear
of free will learning that spat is spawn
of oysters or other shellfish for the love
of fair play a blade is only a tulip
towing the line is a linen
thread through a flaxen rabbit beloved by a long line

a clouded day

oysters stir
the air: where are you
where are you.
if letting the ferret
out hunting the diminutive of pirate
or a similar animal to ferret out big feelings
is saying oysters can continue living as long as nightmares.
a woman walks into a cafe holding a ferret
under her raincoat and it is not a euphemism.
it is only a moon moon remember
a ferret fits itself inside an old oyster shell;
eye could take a little cloud inside.

eye look at black clouds
like clodhopping
hoping to see the oysterman
means pointing the camera lens into the light.
eyeball beside the pewter white
for the love of the shell the shore
fortification for the structural formation
of earth then now working thick.
eye look into black could as seeing flies in season.

entitled days*

ash is fresh wood ashes
and flint

ash grey is white as smoke
and fresh grey
and a very little yellow fishes for grey
and carmine red eye spy a spear tree
read on for fear play

smoke is best of the robin
and flint tile a kind of hard stone

eye spy sparking to ignite touchwood
and smoke is ash mixed
with a mackerel little brown

pearl is back of blackheads
and kitty hawk gulls
and back of petal liver
and petals of purple hepatica
and porcelain jasper pour sell lay down

pearl is ash mixed
with a little crimson read on blue
or blue fishes for grey with a little red read on

yellow fish is vent covering white
and hind end stems for
infinitely many worlds for grey
and stems of barberry
and sanded down calcedony

yellow fishes grey is ash
mixed with lemon yelling out
wait a minute
and a minute portion of brown

blue fish is back
and tail coverts of wood pigeon
overlapping limestone
blue fishes for grey is ash grey mixed
with a little blue blushing
covering to help airflow
overnight and many less worlds
for saying grey is my forever favored color
and he is grey

black fish is back of the nuthatch
and flint tonight

black fishes for grey
is black fishes for pencil lead
without luster is ash
with a little blue blushing
and a portion of black walls beside
I eyeball horses for sale
for something else to feel falling
eyeballs saying fishes fishes we all fall down

*adapted from the entry for grey in Werner's *Nomenclature of Colours: Adapted to Zoology, Botany, Chemistry, Mineralogy, Anatomy, and the Arts* by P. Syme 2nd edition printed for William Blackwood, Edinburgh; and T. Cadell, Strand London. 1821

Note toward Watertight

It says a lot about me that I needed to understand the patterning in a sestina and why the first and last words becoming the last line in the envoi is so satisfying. It feels like a romance to follow the words over many stanzas where they move near and farther apart and yet we know they will end up together. I say this as much as the reader as the writer. The problem, however, is that the sestina pattern does not work for twelve words the way it does for six. Alan R. Champneys, Poul G. Hjorth, and Harry Man explain in great mathematical detail in their article, "The Numbers Lead a Dance: Mathematics of the Sestina" why this is so. The math is mostly beyond me. What matters for the purpose of my project is that they suggest eleven words will yield a sestina and following the algorithm I found that it does with the exception of the envoi. I found the one word final line unsatisfactory, so I added a twelfth word that wandered throughout the stanzas like so many drops of water getting into places where we might not wish them. This wandering word was naturally water. The subject of the poem is the moon snail in the sense that I wanted to play with the idea of two people in a situation approaching each other slowly with similarities and the very real symmetric fear of being attacked, because moon snails will try to eat their own. This is merely a metaphor for forming relationships in middle age. The thing about later in life relationships is that patterns are already made for better or worse and both subjects / moon snails had always lived next to water, mostly salt water. If you are wondering whether or not I ended the sestina with these moon snails getting together the answer is open to interpretation, because I left the reader with the moon and the water. Putting the words moon and snail together felt too obvious and I really didn't want a wandering moon in the poem anyway.

Champneys, Alan, et al., 'The numbers lead a dance: Mathematics of the Sestina,' *Non-linear partial differential equations, mathematical physics, and stochastic analysis: the Helge Holden anniversary volume,* European Mathematical Society. <http://www.bristol.ac.uk/red/research-policy/pure/user-guides/brp-terms/> [Accessed 23 June 2025]

Julia Rose Lewis is a writer. She and Wilfred Franklin wrote together the essay collection, *Overly verbal Ape: Studies in the work of SJ Fowler.* She has authored the poetry collections: *Phenomenology of the Feral* (KFS 2017), *High Erratic Ecology* (KFS 2020), *The Hen Wife* (Contraband 2020), *Misuse* (KFS 2024). She and Nathan Hyland Walker co-authored *The Velvet Protocol* (KFS 2022). She and Paul Hawkins co-authored the visual poetry collection *Postcards From Mental States* (Hesterglock Press 2023). She has published ten pamphlets, the most recent of which is *Still Life* (Storybox Collective 2025).

Jeff Harrison

Birds, Lakes, and Observations

splits unchipped, chips unsplit
counting threw beauty, followed night beauty
stitch gutter mountains, glossy proof of days' injuries

corpses' thief winds up in the fallen minute moors
wrong our bright voluptuously open heads
new me is the shine, you're my night

Virginia prefers birds,
lakes, and observations to
the spiteful riddles of my tongue

bite it back, slash what steps feet don't like
careful, lest Wormswork sewer the stars, lakes, and roses

Jeff Harrison has publications from *Writers Forum, Persistencia Press*, and *Furniture Press*. He has e-books from *BlazeVOX* and *Argotist Ebooks*. His poetry has appeared in *An Introduction to the Prose Poem* (Firewheel Editions), *Noon: An Anthology of Short Poems* (Isobar Press), three *Meritage Press* hay(na)ku anthologies, *Sentence: a Journal of Prose Poetics, Otoliths, Moria, Word For Word*, and elsewhere.

Kathryn Rantala

Ghost Fish of the Estuary

Holes

pillory or host

for chips

shells

tenants

the smalls in peat

in tide

in attitudes of

prayer

beneath a wing a nest

no fish

each or west

ground still breathing

*

silt water sun moon

kiln

a bright round wound

august

neither stops

nor soon

*

if this were now

it would be

transformation

if I were writing

but

I am

I post myself in air

text me

Letter North (5)

Barnacles
the patent/
patient moss
siphons water
eats paint
and under
dark rotates with
the earth I know

I row and row

parts of day delineated
by loon
bullhead
fish
intermittent harm

by night

campfires lethal

as warm

heart

indifferent to span

largely

missing

no pity in it

Moorage Rules: The Painter

. Painters are for tethering or drawing

. Painters are particular by boat

. Do not drag the painter in the water; do not
pull so hard the knot goes tight; do not loosen
knots with knives

I ask

is where you are now

still how far

we come

for beauty

Bio: Kathryn Rantala's recent collection, *My Archipelago*, a finalist for the 2024 Big Other Award for Poetry, was published by Sandy Press. Her chap, *Down by the Humus Lake,* is forthcoming in On the Seawall, and she has an illustrated essay in an upcoming anthology on Feminism and AI from Louffa Press. Her collaboration with Camano Island, Washington, artist Jack Gunter, *The Gunter Series*, appeared in 2024 and, in 2023, Spuyten Duyvil published her collection of prose poetry *A Little Family*. She is also an assemblage/sculpture artist, with work in juried art shows throughout the Cascadia region. Her website is kathrynrantala.com.

Olchar E. Lindsann

Leavy Breaksaft

  doe-frost trotting
puck thru trade insider
rest un-rustle page
that bone clan's flick;
  munch corpus moss
stock faun needle slopes
habeus rummage petals
pale graze bus flaming;
  sandman cud contagious
mistletoe my cauldron's ire
guided troth to epic
meter tanking holey missal.

Hous*ing* Blade

"Alone pus at river."
      – *Popol Vuh.*

*n*ever, nor mal nectar's
gust slab cur*rent:* p*ill*
*b*last k*ether,* p*lush* of fester,
jaguar ch*amber* microchip,
contagion made in chin, a
n*ether* whirled in stealth, a scope,
a mal kuth b*oil* patent feather
rubber riot c*rank*shaft pope;
all vulgar lance sh*ill* vector's
settler colon eyes, sewn closed.

135

seFaire Safari

~~~>*<~~>*<~~~~~~~~~~~~~~

"urning I fired two shots at par
rots. I reloaded the gun aft"
– Scott MacLeod, *Unholy Union*.

~~~~~~~~~~~~~~~~>*<~~>*<~~~

gravid
on eht melted archipelago
nerve mistook yr bullet eyeface slat for catalyptic shredding,
ere ye toppled
maw all choked with cop batons
in retcon flending fowl recorded coils,
looms of wove complacencies, right there on screen, racoon
of plague betides our nostrum
anvil bile anodyne,
a bombed-out child
broach hotel, awaft with xerographic plumage
hocked up gulag squirms eht gaster,
drone rot burst speared pure upon eht porcupine.

Leviathan inViolante

a *st*ride o'er the scorch
mal lignum, zombied civit
as *sc*raping-sky as bulkbarrage; be
hold: vast *s*talking-knot of fascistinated
ghola masses in si*n'ew*-t'wisted classtaclysm
*sw*eating poison pollis plague
archon cyclopean, meatmount of spi*ritch*oke; *h*ail
our ubu spectre hulker nero, headbag-counter,
citieszin-leveller flatline go'lieth,
his haollowed head in 3G drone-buzz halo strike
his shadow teeming proxy genosideline
magog gorged on greyflesh *f*lakes of pauper; lo
his rib packed prison bars of vegestated sense; lo
his b'rain of skull, usurper's*hell*, b*st*one tyrannic

tugs galvanic on droned billions on w*ire*less of Adam*ant*
    tearr,or a mal gamaeted puppest; lo
his eyes snake gleams panoptic, hi-def bureaucrasatellite; lo
his spittle missiles children mince. groan, be
neathis weight of ordin*ance*ary, rattle empty death, be
*tend*ons organs resignated cells to clout consolidant:
        th'mammoth thug of mammon
        th'under-dealer of death's *dis*count
        father of phosphor nations.

Olchar E. Lindsann has published nearly 50 books of literature, theory, translation, and avant-garde history including six books of the ongoing multi-volume avant-epic poem *Arthur Dies* (Luna Bisonte Prods). His poems have appeared in *Otoliths, Lost & Found Times, BlazeVOX, Brave New Word,* and elsewhere, his essays in *No Quarter, Slova, & Fifth Estate*; and he has performed sound poetry and lectured extensively. He is the editor of *mOnocle-Lash Anti-Press*, whose catalog includes over 200 print publications of the contemporary and historical avant-garde, and of the periodicals *Rêvenance, Synapse*, and *The in-Appropriated Press*. He translates work of the French avant-garde of the 19th & early 20th centuries.

Sara Greenslit

MLF

1. At first it seems overly tidy, a neat dozen—12 sets of nerves that originate from your brain, the cranial nerves, with their orderly matching right and left sides. These nerves control our ability to smell, see, move our eyes, swallow, taste, hear, balance, cry, salivate, and even feel sensation to our face and mouth as well as move our mouth muscles to make a grin, a grimace, a kiss.

2. One, the vagus nerve, number 10, CN X, the "wandering" nerve, leaves the brainstem, travels down the neck and chest to innervate our viscera—sending messages from the gut back to the brain. It does a multitude of other things, like influencing heart rate, controlling muscles of the larynx so we can speak, helping us sweat, and creating a muscle wave in the intestines, peristalsis, so that our food goes down and not up.

3. In first year anatomy lab, we made a goofy mnemonic to remember whether each nerve function was sensory, motor or both: *Some Say Money Matters But Marlon Brando Says Big Boobies Matter Most,* which I inscribed in pen on the back pages of my Evan's and deLahunta's *Guide to the Dissection of the Dog.*

4. I also have a sticker that says *Way to Go!* on the inside front cover to cheer me through a tough first semester. The mnemonic for the names of nerves, well, it's dirty, go look it up yourself.

5. Cranial nerve one, CN I, is for smelling, olfaction. My grandfather sustained a head injury from a tree—he afterward over-salted his food (no smell, no taste), scolding his wife for making it too bland.

6. Our CN I isn't terrific, but a dog's—magnify what you are able to smell by twenty times more scent receptors, and the world flowers and flourishes and astounds with rich and layering perfumes.

7. But this organization rarely leads to an immediate, clear-cut diagnosis when neurological problems appear. An old Labrador falling and circling to one side, and head tilted in the same direction, not able to stand, drink or defecate: is it stroke, brain tumor, ear infection, or unknown?

8. The MLF, medial longitudinal fasciculus, is a pair of symmetrical nerve tracts leaving the brain stem, coordinating three eye muscles nerves, CN III, IV, VI, the oculomotor, trochlear and abducens. These nerves allow you to move your eye, from up and down to a full out eye roll.

9. This tract also connects to your balance system, an intertwined and complicated coordination of input from the cerebellum, neck and eye muscle movements, inner ear organs (saccule and utricle, that measure acceleration and angular motion), CN VIII, the vestibulocochlear nerve, and muscle fibers in ankles and feet. The tract runs both ways: input to and from the brain, always measuring how and when you move.

10. So it made sense that I got dizzy while using a microscope, driving a car, reading text on a computer, scrolling through CT images. My eye movements were hooked into the balance apparatus, and it wasn't clear which part was damaged.

11.

12. *You spin me round round, like a record, round—*

Sara Greenslit is a small animal veterinarian from Wisconsin. She earned an MFA in poetry from Penn State and a DVM from the University of Wisconsin-Madison. She has published two hybrid novels, *As If A Bird Flew By Me*, winner of the FC2 Sukenick Innovative Fiction Award, and *The Blue of Her Body*, winner of the Starcherone Prize for Innovative Fiction. Her essays have appeared in *Fourth Genre, Hobart, Cordella, Western Humanities Review, Kestrel, Gold Wake Live, Bat City* and *Rupture*.

John Olson

A Life In Words

I yelled at everybody "wake up Pop I floated." Just now. Too quick
for anyone to notice. I'm chronically hungry for validation. I water
it with flutes. I aim sharply into artifice to ponder a lure. Our
agitations are immaterial given the auspices of a spoon. There's no
mock hunger in my catalogue. It's all burner plates and lingerie. I
soaked a sigh in gin above a smooth vermouth and gave it a life in
words. You can build a whimsical seminary during your
whereabouts. Growing beans is slightly more difficult, but the
results are sleeping. You can do a loop on the cubes in addition to
getting anything. I'm enthralled right now with your attention to
these things. I spared this moment to gurgle your republic this
many meanings ago. I don't know if you could feel it, but if you
did, there are myriad lumps of charcoal spawned by a half-light in
a west side basement. Nothing is perfect and that's the beauty of it.
We're up to our eyeballs in cactus. The medication is beginning to
take effect, like moonlight in silk. It's difficult to clearly express
one's dissatisfaction with something. Especially if that something
is drapery. It's what I live for.

My Belief In Stucco

Consciousness is punctured by the prick of the elliptical and
coagulates in language. Dawn plus stars equals exaltation. It can
happen when you least expect it. There are spheres in which one
may freely skulk around in despair, soliloquies with which to flirt
with gingivitis. Always bring a toothbrush. Wherever you go.
Don't let despair get in the way of your logistics. Hygiene is to
hovels what hovels are to novels: they put everything in higher
definition. Healthy teeth and healthy gums can excuse myriad
buckets of risible faux pas. If you ever find yourself in an
aerodrome with a beautiful lobster and a portrait of Milton Berle
you might consider flying that fork of baklava right into your
mouth. More things have happened to me in bed than ever

occurred in college. I remember a motel room in Moab. Sipping a can of beer while listening to thunder echo through an amphitheater of hoodoos. Bob Dylan and Tom Petty on TV. A mosquito above a glittering architecture of beer and iodine. I felt a blast of autonomy rise within me, and held on tight to the table as paroxysms of pure conjecture shook my belief in stucco.

I went to a Halloween party once as The Invisible Man, à la Claude Rains in a trench coat and slouch hat, a swath of bandages wrapped around his head for visibility. It so disturbed a book distributor and coke dealer that I was encouraged to remove it. The bandages, at least. And sunglasses. Let's not forget those. I carried a tiny notebook at the time, filled with consonants in a whorl of troubling simulacrums. When I went to the bathroom Frankenstein was taking a bubble bath. I told him about that scene in Hard Day's Night when Lennon is taking a bath and his manager pulls the plug and the water drains and he ain't there. Frankenstein (the monster, not Victor, the crazy, sociopathic scientific genius that brought him into life) said nothing. I pulled the plug and he disappeared. Life is full of appearances and disappearances. It's why Cubism looks so choppy in the middle of a hammered bottle. It's all about fragments and angles. I think it's why I feel so antisocial whenever I'm gazing at an appliance. Dials equal control, and control equals madness. The electricity goes wild. The monster's fingers move. It's alive! It's alive!

Independence exhumes my notebook of effusion. I'm bigger when I'm brief. The twang of the guitar haunts the drapery as it swings on a hinge of flippancy. This makes the room bigger. What ghost thrives on absorption? In consciousness the piano rolls right through you. It doesn't stop when the note is askew. Deviation is the embodiment of intrigue. It's best to plan your escape before the light of day steals the darkness. I open a catalogue of tornados and agree to spin my skin in spirals next time I exercise. If I can't explain my emotions, who can? And is it worth the bother? I achieved manhood in a culture of astronauts and crazy brassieres. I knew a cat burglar once who didn't steal for money, he stole for the adrenalin rush. Feel the breeze? I opened a window. The morning is back and it feels athletic. The sidewalk is long and laughing. If you've never heard concrete laugh, you're missing out on a splendor of cracks. One day I want to do an anthology of poems composed in the fog. Strains of Bizet. Syllables of ice. Mallarmé on a train.

The music is a description I spooned with indigo. I dreamed of a baptism of loons. The smell of consciousness in upheaval. Wet, bawdy, tender. Eyes in a long stare at the stars outside Tucson. Should I chew another antacid? Calcium Carbonate. I don't want another kidney stone. The pain was unmanageable. It equals giving birth, is what women say. Diagnosis can be tough. Look for symptoms. Do the examination after a mood of audacity prowls through you. That soulful sound of silk in Lucinda William's voice evinces a history of pain. Have you ever watched a woman wrestle her way out of a rope on a Devil's Wheel in München, Germany during Octoberfest? Different context, different kind of pain. But it goes to my central point, which is still spinning, still struggling to resolve its issues with a degree of grace. Like that moment I was invited to play with the Rolling Stones, and as the curtain raised, I shouted to Keith hey! I don't know how to play a guitar! What do I do? And he handed me something to swallow. Which I did. And then I woke up and it was morning and two women were talking about extraterrestrial life, antimatter, prototaxites and Homo sapiens. It was a lot to take in. What's a prototaxite? Let's start there. A prototaxite is a terrestrial fossil fungi dating from the Late Silurian to the Late Devonian periods, approximately 430 to 360 million years ago. Ok, then. I get it now. It's endless. No end in sight. Just a long deserted gas station and the silhouette of David Lynch walking out of an eyeball.

Podium Poem

To one day stand at a podium and confess that I, too, am sometimes bashful in front of my biology would be an act of such great disproportion as to constitute a parallel immodesty. Reality, without articulation, tends to break. We find pieces of it everywhere. Bubbles, deviations, gold. My fingers wrestle and twist in front of my stomach. There are so many things to pick up and caress. Even the rest stops offer a modicum of rumor. Things we never expected is a sure sign of work. Ok, then. We'll get down

143

to it. The sheer absence of any certitude keeps us company out on the highway. Next time you're in the shower think about Heidegger. And hammers and nails. Things that make sense. Dab what the skin has learned from the glockenspiel. Soft pale fingers on a piano keyboard. After all, clouds perform a service. They bring rain. They bring suitcases full of thunder. I hear the garden hose hissing in the pipes of the building. It makes me think of greyhounds. Grommets, sometimes. Scream parachute next time you fall out of a mirror to reflect this. My art is based on a concept of Bohemia. It's dynamic to think a breast has metaphorical properties. One sometimes finds grace in the honey of rapport. That a language can harbor a stream of misdirections in a single compliment is nothing less than fluffy. Maybe that's why I never get along with cameras. I'm too quick to cop a feel. Sometimes it's better to hold back than jump ahead. I like it when a sentence evolves out of nothing and inflates with the moment, gaping at the wonder of it all, every line a vine, every word a grape.

The Chaos Of Neglected Rain

It's kind of weird. You sit here and you think to yourself, what's going to happen? And then it hits you with full force: Baudelaire preferred laudanum. The luxuries of the intellect. This is where I began to wonder if I really understood Dion. For example, when he sang "I go through life without a care / 'Til I'm as happy as a clown /With my two fists of iron and I'm going nowhere." Does that sound like something Nietzsche might've written? In the end one loves one's desire and not what is desired. Ok. Fair enough. I have a humor eager to do some brushwork. It was night now, and there was a soft glow coming from the Dancing Ganesha.

Abandoned by the museum, I wriggled free of the diorama and disappeared into the nearby woods. Our senses never entirely learn to be subtle. Hypnosis is itself a marginal aloofness. This is where the malleability of Being comes into play. Contrasting colors and bohemian artists and dachshunds. Who wouldn't want to see a cardboard rocket explode from somebody's throat? I know I would.

I remember a woman in mink who stood by a jukebox in St. Louis waiting to hear Julie London sing "Cry Me A River." You'd be surprised at the number of cities with rivers running through them. Or lonely women or lonely men. Bars where Chuck Berry used to hang out. The skill it takes to impart a sentiment at the right time and the right place. You should glaze your metaphysics with a brushbefore announcing the gateway to paradise. No one likes a messy attic. The chaos of neglected rain. Spider webs. Raw memories. Wandering eyes.

There are different meanings that attach to the stirring of a philodendron. It is so much easier to approximate rather than contemplate a tree, much less a philodendron. The crackle under the log has ultimate authority. If there's something shadowy and vague in the room you'd like to capture in words, go ahead. Be my guest. Frame it, make it flowery, indent it. Don't spit against the wind. Blow the salt across the table. Slam the door on the way out. The scarf puffs out with the breeze. There's some highway work taking place near a swamp. The slow big road is a fierce articulation of rapid decisions. The hammer is not a sensual object, but it does contain a genie. It comes out when we pound things, nails, mostly, which jingle in paper bags when you bring them home, and plunk them in the toolbox. The genie is all these things. The service it performs for us in gratitude for releasing it from the hammer, is to bind the spines in the library with legible gold.

We store our feelings in alphabets, letters chiseled from the surrounding air, like hooks on a storage rack. Our feelings about victory, vicissitude, the arbitrary immodesties of history. Our feelings about one another. Our feelings about sex, seclusion, digestion, spirituality and work. Spaghetti. Labor unions. Goldfish. Hunger. The price of eggs. The anatomy of rain. Heidegger's hammer. The universe. And, of course, its chaos. The birth and death of stars. Cataclysmic change triggered by asteroids. Idiot politicians. Crazed industrialists. Fascist oligarchs. The death of solitude. The solitude of death. Meaning is quieter now. It hangs in the existential closet like an old winter coat from a more meaningful past. It needs a new zipper and the pockets have holes in them. But it emanates intimacy with a time and a place that felt far more negotiable and fun. It's more memory than coat. What it coats is nebulous. Not necessarily vague, but divorced from the banalities of the moment. The sleeves hang empty, but their reach is longer.

The sadness of the chicken is not the same as the sadness of the rhinoceros. Sadness isn't a hug. There is no general sadness. The sadness that comes from the summits of mountains weighs on the soul like the literature of things still unwritten. It's a very particularspecies of sadness. It's the sadness of hawks and circus performers. Acrobats, mainly. The sadness of acrobats deepens when pretending to be tough and defiant in the face of high risks and human connections. The sadness of mountain peaks is padlocked in bad motel art. Mountain climbers generally feel euphoric on the summits of mountains, confident and validated and fantastically ennobled, purified by the extreme effort of attaining a peak and the redeeming energy of sacrifice. The sadness arrives later, in the harsh light of a divorce proceeding. Sadness occupies the middle of the emotional spectrum. At the far-right end is the crushing iron of grief. Invincible, immutable, and non-negotiable. At the far left is the rapture of catastrophe, the ecstasies of lust and the triumph of will. Extreme states stimulated by fantastical circumstances. And that's just sad.

Yo-Yo

Experience is equivalent to art by means of lines, colors, movements, dreams and drunkenness. Howling mountainous waves. Delirium and tremulous rhythms. The blissful ecstasy that rises whenever a play of colors before the eyes functions as the prerequisite of all Dionysian impulse, a signal paganism centered in extravagant sexual licentiousness, and song and pantomime. Extreme states of inebriation often result in brutal insights. Now the slave is free, ready to live life and its steady flow, as the musical mirror of the world refills our glass with lyrical splendor. Art was born of need. Shadows on the wall. Picture sparks all around manifesting a power quite unknown. Depictions in greasy syntax. Reality as it is in itself, the whole Divine Comedy of Life, violently stirred into a shimmering substance of string. A yo-yo spinning in the air.

Until Leeuwenhoek ground his marvelous lenses, I had no idea how much bacteria raised a ruckus around our health, for good or bad, teeming at that delicate boundary between the organic and inorganic, pointing to levels of cognition beyond all phenomena, refining, combining, mutating, manipulating destinies and enhancing the stew of life with the seasoning of decrepitude and decay. Subjective factors of emotion appear as yet unsatisfied. Such cells are said to be eukaryotic. Even when language is stirred to its utmost, there remain materials and energies outside the body that like to hang on walls and dazzle people with peacocks and old barns. Sometimes a poem or story will indicate that our innermost beings are partly cause and partly effect. The cause of primary spermatocytes, the effect of messy conjunctions, and drops of pond water. The end result may be folds of impasto, or a mirror in the belly of an African fetish.

Skin is the part of the body in contact with the external environment, reveling in the mud or jetting down a ski slope in a James Bond movie, or sitting still, modeling for an artist in the Paris of the 1890s, pondering a book as your form assumes life on a canvas, usually thick enough that the brush or painting-knife strokes are visible. Sometimes, when we fold inward to greet our demands, and see ourselves in embryonic development, the tenor of our actual life may come across as preoccupied, maybe a little peculiar, where the warm poetry of our thoughts forms a bulging protuberance on our outer manifestation, scooping ice cream from a freezer for a group of teenage girls. Need, labor, and matter are like the façade of a religious edifice, prosodies in stone full of enjoyed meanings. Our biologies are highways in the realm of allegory, contractions of the epididymis doodled in neon asterisks. About the time the ovum erupts, a new meaning crawls into the world, unheeded but full of treasure, a spear tipped with a pine cone.

What is beauty, we all wonder about that, it seems to be disappearing, even the notion of it has lost its former pertinence. All previous attempts at absolutes failed in abject hosiery. Gym socks and Eleusinian symbolism. What then is this conception of form people have, this idea of pressing buttons in elevators to go up or down? Does anybody think of going sideways? Why are there no buttons for going sideways in elevators? Sometimes a quandary can be ornamental, the mystery of perception liberated from the excesses of realism. This is why experience comes before explanation. Pressing the button for Hollywood makes the doors slide wide open to a spectacle of chorus dancers dressed in spangled gold costumes. Devices of any sort can be powerful adjuncts for our fulfillment as we quietly percolate the fluids of the universe. As soon as one sits down to write, there sometimes comes a shiver, a naked woman rising out of the sea on a clam shell. What I can tell you is that she loves Ritz crackers. What I can't tell you is why.

John Olson is the author of numerous books of poetry and prose poetry, including *Echo Regime, Free Stream Velocity, Backscatter: New and Selected Poems, Larynx Galaxy, Dada Budapest*, and *Weave of the Dream King*. He was the recipient of the The Stranger's 2004 Literature Genius Award, and in 2012 was one of eight finalists for the Washington State Arts Innovator Award. He has also published five novels, including *Souls of Wind* (shortlisted for The Believer Book Award, 2008), *The Nothing That Is, The Seeing Machine, In Advance of the Broken Justy,* and *Mingled Yarn,* an autofiction. *You Know There's Something*, his 6th novel, was published by Grand Iota Press in May, 2023. A 7th novel – *Unfinished World–* will be published soon this summer by Quale Press.

As for my writing, there are two central principles that inspire my work: Zuihitsu, a Japanese literary genre characterized by a highly fluid, personal, and often fragmented style, resembling a stream of consciousness or a pyrotechnic chrysanthemum bursting outward in ecstatic arbitrary arcs. A Big Bang on a sheet of paper. Zuihitsu essays often begin with one theme, a specific event, a single idea, a stroll down the street, an item in the news, and then allow it to morph into whatever happens to be inspired by the initial statement, so that the author is often surprised with the direction the writing might take. The second principle is an idea spawned by French anthropologist Claude Levi-Strauss, which he called the "floating signifier." A floating signifier is a word or symbol that has a vague or undefined meaning, allowing it to be filled with various interpretations and symbolic values. It essentially acts as a placeholder that can be filled with different signifieds (meanings) by different individuals or within different contexts. The master of this technique is Stephane Mallarmé, particularly his prose poems, such as "Music and Letters," inspired by a talk he gave at Oxford in 1894.

Jeff Bagato

guidelines

    block or limit

   consent.   reasons
       ensure compliance

   language customer

such blocking

    limitation access or
       compliance

   case of cross
    sure effects

forms

    accords

       effects
access effects

If those aren't the reasons, what
      are the reasons

gallant playbook

    frozen. a mile
       climbed to business

freet afield ablest

    journey and this
        journey

a day in the business
    a day in the mines

you look, no
    you look

keys taken
    keys returned

if those aren't the keys,
   what are the keys?

times like this. a better
    regard

jade slick
    rather that test
      missed abatement

gradual. kind. feeling it out
    slope engine

wallet empty or full

a problem. pour
    salt in the wounds

slip. doling it out
  a problem precious
    get behind
  a tracker,
      trial
  affirmation

guestimate banter

  an entry designed
    for greatness

bezel delight

    zigzag fresh at
          once
      patent a ladder

        ward aloof signal

oh those magic
        days of youth,
    again
          a star
  at every door, step
        lively

land of plenty
      and all
    that

right again

        stack magic
     again in the
         zone

blade lout parse
    access toll

   what carp feed on
    what bless
  feels like

    wading
   attraction backward

bold little find

   a skill
  through a pastiche/
    pastille/
    pastime /
    pasture /
   smells like
  sargassum at sea

try again label,
   try again

Jeff Bagato produces poetry and prose as well as mail art, electronic music and glitch video. His latest books document experimental text work from the past few years, including *In the Engine Room with Bettie and Andrea Reading Pornography, Gonch Poems, Robot Speak,* and *Floral Float Flume: Flue Flit Flip.* A blog about his writing and publishing efforts can be found at http://jeffbagato.wordpress.com.

Bob Lucky

A Day at the Museum

I remember a security guard holding a phone
close to his face with one hand and twirling
in the other an unlit cigarette like a baton

    as I strolled through galleries
    admiring the walls.

By the time I got to the second floor
I couldn't remember why I was there
or what I had seen.

    In the gift shop
    I bought an unruled notebook

to remind me of my day at the museum.
Outside, the guard was smoking a cigarette,
blowing clouds of smoke through a mustache
I'll never forget. Salvador Dalí would die again
for a mustache like that.

Parenting

His parents weren't happy with him digging a hole in the back
yard.
What the hell are you doing, his father demanded to know.
He lobbed a shovelful of dirt out of the hole and said,
I'm going to China. I'm tired of this place. I want
fireworks and dragons. His mother would bring
him a sandwich in the evenings and ask when
he was coming in to do his homework.
Education is important, she would
stress. This is my life's work, he
would say. They made a bit

of cash selling all the dirt
their son tossed up.
Eventually they
lost touch but
learned a bit
of Chinese
just in
case.

The Agnostic's Prayer
    after Nissim Ezekiel

O my imaginary friend
all I ask of you
is a hamburger and a beer
and the sudden death
of a fascist or two
(natural causes of course)

Do your best

The city is beautiful
after days of rain
the empty churches
soaking up the sun

I am grateful
for some things

A Scene from My Life as an Action Movie

I'm captured by my demons and interrogated. They tie me to a chair and throw questions and punches at me. Some of the questions are hard; I lie a lot or make things up when I don't know the answer.
Mistaking a pat on the cheek for a sense of humor, I try to be funny. It isn't funny. During a coffee break, I ask the demons some questions, but they don't know any more than I do.

Full Stop

I wasnt too concerned when the last exclamation point faded away. Just the extinction of yet another needless punctuation mark. Now however the period is following in the footprints of commas & apostrophes & all the dashes hyphen en & em. Ironically its being temporarily replaced by the ellipsis. O the irony. The ampersand is making a comeback. Economics I suppose one or two fewer strokes on the keyboard depending on if *and* is capitalized or not. of course capitalization is also on its last legs (unlike cliches and parentheses) not a big loss but the loss of the period may create some confusion in one area the space between one sentence and another. what i'm afraid of is that when the last period disappears i wont be able to stop writing...i mean i may have to keep going until i run out of words but then ill just make up some more even though im too old to traipse through the garden like adam & eve naming everything i see reinvent the wheel before the wheel has even been invented...

Bob Lucky is the author most recently of *Careful Not to Startle the Yaks* (Cyberwit, 2025) and My *Wife & Other Adventures* (Red Moon Press, 2024), winner of the HSA Merit Book Award for best haibun collection 2024. His work has appeared in *Rattle, Otoliths,*

MacQueen's Quinterly, Unlost, Contemporary Haibun, Utriculi, and other publications. He lives in Portugal.

Stacey Allam

Sugary

Weeding out
Sweet movements
Of advantages
Of not thinking
In thoughts
Pinpointed
Going with the
Flow
Of the sweet embroidery
That did all of this
To me

Smoothing

There was no
Chunk of chocolate
For her
To scrape
Her tooth
Against
So she just
Straightened
Out her skirt
Blew the balloon
Up
And had
A nice
Day

He didn't
Want the fans
Edges
To hit his
Tousled hair
While doing
Anything else
Buttoning his
Lip
Paying no attention
To all the
Buttoned up
Tuxedoes
Playing
Over there

The tullips
Bloomed sideways
Shredding off
The candy wrapper
Leaving the bar
Naked
On the highway
Not knowing
Which end
Is up

The constant
Movement
Of the advantages
Of not thinking
In thoughts
Did all of this
To her

Stacey Allam. I have been writing my whole life minus the time I was a baby. I am currently 64 years old. I have been been published in many small press publications such as lost and found times through luna bisonte productions. My books are *All Those Connected Pathways Nostril of a Muscle Cloud,* and *Tongue Tickling.* The last two books mentioned were collaborative efforts of John M Bennett and myself. I currently reside in Brooklyn NY with my husband my son and my pet cat bon bon.

John M. Bennett

el amor espejadoodajepse

I   am dis   olving in h   ir
?   s   a
revolves a foglost c   air a dri   ing
                        h   p
                                    p
thr   at s   d mis di   ntes   n a   ua
   o   e   e   e   g
si   pi   l sin b   rbote   r al l   do
   n   e   o   a   a
del a   or de mi   tr   wh   is me
      m   o o   o
no   m   el yo el o   ro del ot   o
      t   e   t   r
que   s o soy is not me is   s   s
      e   e   i
yo es you is ti youesyoisti itsioyseuoy

finger stain throats the alley
   -For CMB

transubstantiation of air to ink
my fingers' b lack my tongue
a b lank breeze bl ack air was
writ me you *scrawled d d d   d   it*
 "3 rocks on a log" knew the ● ● ●
answer , lost the answ...   a
toothless comb in the alley's weeds

          ⊓

frigorífico

mis sueños de piedra me
cobran . un título infil
trado con ácido dulce
, un agua refrita con
aire . es mi lengua bífida
, tu ojo pintado al revés
que me ve como nada o
algo , un alga que me
crece en tu pulmón circ
ular , circular como si
vacío   fuere . . . . .   .
si la luz vacía fuere si
mi cara el viento ~ ~ ~
se despertare
nunca
en nuca

in he dead window's swirl

●

silencio   o viento ~~~ , iguales
son , ~●~ mi boca stuffed with
toothpaste my crumpled voices dia
lects   stones   splinters   cilensio
que me oye   legs   twit ching in
dark sheets where yr grave l d rifts a
cloud tunnel ☻ ☻☻☻☻☻ my
hands s crawled with tiny cuts / \ _ \ >
                    spell ....dust

                .   .

                .   .

                ....

                shit dessication
                caca ciega
                🌢

John M. Bennett's instruction and motto to himself as an artist
and poet is: BE BLANK

Jack Galmitz

Exception

Words are what exist between
the falling rain and the street.

In the suffused light that appears
whenever the sky is dark, they are not there.

In the rumble of wheels on cobble stones
bound to the market with fresh produce,
there is not a single thought.

The busy street is like an oil painting
by Luigi Loir; everything is present but nothing
is distinct. You will find there no measured feet.

Then two boys emerge from around
an arch passing a ball back and forth
and one of them shouts "look out"
as a car turns sharply past.

Interpretation

The night was cold. I wrapped myself in blankets
and took with me a book to read about lovers.

I hoped this would keep me warm.
It was a book of verses by the poets of Provence and written in
earnest.

At first, I set my heart too high on one
who had been the consort of the Dove,

but she rebuffed me. I was too coarse and common
like a hopsack suit for service. I turned to another more suitable for
me.

Soon after, I declared my love for her a flower
and hoped she would preserve me in her waters.

I slept fitfully all night as I sailed on roiling waters.
Before I woke to my familiar surroundings,
she returned my feelings and fulfilled my yearnings.

The day crawled quietly along the wall
as the shadow of all outdoors.

The Meaning of the Story

It is surprised by the sudden appearance of a river
and a young couple sitting by its shore watching
the currents. It had no idea in advance they were coming.
Nor did it know there would be stones that made
white water or that there were dead tree limbs across it.
There is a great blue heron on a tree above it that rests
the sun on its wings for comfort. Two
young men in a canoe suddenly cut through its tensions.
It is calmed by this moment. It is the purpose of it.

The water is deep and dark. You cannot see the bottom
if there is one. It bends around a tall shale wall
and arrives at an odor so foul it would turn back if it could.
A tannery built a century before is nestled in trees
along the bank. The water there is murky, green with chemicals
and flesh. It gallops on like a colt nevertheless
for there is so much more river to it
and it is curious of itself.

Cut Outs
(for Henri Matisse)

"Art should be something like a good armchair in which to rest
from physical fatigue."
Certainly, art should be. And art should be something.
Art should be good, never indifferent.
Art should always be like, never exactly.
Art should be a rest in a long journey.
Art should be a window a black cat looks out of constantly.
Art should be physically stimulating.
Art should be multi-dimensional.
Color liberates the child.
The colors should be simple and animal.
I would not mind turning into a vermillion goldfish, Matisse said.
He made a painting of his studio all in red.
During the war, he developed cancer.
He spent his remaining years in a wheelchair.
He painted with scissors from then.
He called them cut outs and assembled them.
He suffered from fatigue.
He never lost love.
He saw flowers everywhere and said everyone could.
That was who he was.

Jack Galmitz was born in New York City in 1951. The city he
was born in has long since perished from the earth. He graduated
with a Ph.D from the University of Buffalo. He was a long-time
contributor to Otoliths. His work has appeared in many print and
digital poetry journals, among them *Synchronized Chaos, Alien
Buddha, Ginyu*, a Japanese Journal published by the poet Ban'ya
Natuishi, and *Roadrunner Haiku*, to name a few. He is married and
lives with his wife in New York City in a converted factory
building along a railroad. You get used to it.

George Myers Jr.

A Mosaic (on My DNA, AI and Indeterminacy)

I sing the body electric — and here's the seduction. Make no mistake: it *is* seduction. You can teach AI to decode your writer's DNA — that ineffable something that makes your sentences yours — and then watch it spin new work in your voice. Your ghost in the machine, speaking back to you.

Sometimes you'll want it to. Sometimes, as I found, it will surprise you into wanting it.

But to understand what this means, let's begin where we should: with lineage.

Lineage: Dada, Data, and the French Connection

AI, especially generative AI like ChatGPT, operates in a probabilistic space. It doesn't produce a single, fixed meaning but samples from vast distributions of possibility. Each output is a recombination, a chance encounter of words and phrases — much like Breton's sewing machine and umbrella on a dissecting table.

Experimental poetry — Dada, Oulipo, Surrealism — lives in that same space. Both AI and experimental poetry embrace indeterminacy as both method and meaning.

Marjorie Perloff reminds us: "We cannot really come to terms with the major poetic experiments occurring in our own time without some understanding of what we might call 'the French connection' — the line that goes from Rimbaud to Stein, Pound and Williams by way of Cubist, Dada, and early Surrealist art."

Continuity disguised as rupture. That's what links Duchamp's readymades to GPT's misheard prompts, what binds Mac Low's chance structures to machine-generated verse. AI feels less like revolution, more like the next verse in a poem we've been writing for a century.

Multiplicity, Play and the Fragment

Where the lyric once sought the perfectly chosen word, AI — like postmodern poetry — generates multiple, shifting possibilities. Its output is not final statement but invitation: to curate, to frame, to shape what might otherwise be noise.

Think of Mac Low's index cards, Cage's I Ching-generated scores, Carson's fragmented mourning in *Nox*. AI joins this lineage — another player in the chance orchestra.

And today? Nick Montfort's *Taroko Gorge*, an endlessly generating nature poem written as a simple code loop, remixed by dozens of poets and coders. Allison Parrish's *Articulations*, machine-generated poetic lines that explore phonetic pattern over semantic sense. Ross Goodwin's *1 the Road*, an AI-assisted novel generated during a cross-country road trip — a modern *On the Road* composed by digital co-driver.

Ask AI for a poem: one time you'll get Rilkean depth, another time TikTok slang. Like a Cubist portrait, AI shows language from all angles at once — fractured, layered, polyvocal. On the road.

Intertextuality and the Remix

AI generates language by remixing patterns learned from millions of texts — intertextuality on hyperdrive. Like postmodern pastiche or citation-rich experimental work (Stein's echoing phrases, Pound's layered allusions), AI always speaks in borrowed voices.

Today's artists lean into this. *Obvious* generated Edmond de Belamy, a portrait synthesized from a dataset of historical paintings, sold at Christie's — a Duchampian gesture in code. Lillian-Yvonne Bertram trains models on their own poetry, creating recursive, self-sampling work that rethinks the boundaries of authorship. The remix *is* the message.

Glitch Poetics

AI's oddities — its awkward phrasings, strange analogies, moments of nonsense — aren't defects. They place it squarely within the glitch poetics of the experimental tradition.

Think of Jhave Johnston's *ReRites*, daily machine-generated poems edited by a human hand, the raw glitch left visible like scaffolding.

Like Mac Low's chance compositions or Cage's indeterminate scores, AI reminds us: all language is improvisation.

The glitch is the gift.

Authorship, Ghosts and Frames

Postmodernism long questioned the boundary between author and text, originality and appropriation. AI intensifies that tension.

When it writes in "your voice," who's speaking? The author? The machine? The culture? The collage of training data?

Like Duchamp's readymades, AI's outputs force us to reconsider authorship and intent. The meaning isn't in creation alone, but in selection, framing, curation.

AI's authorship feels like the ultimate extension of Barthes '"death of the author" — the text as a site of multiple readings, generated by chance more than genius.

Code-Switching: Between Intention and Accident

By day, I code-switch for work — navigating brand voices, styles, tones that aren't mine. By night, I prompt the machine, and it code-switches, too — not for identity, but because its stochastic dice demand it.

Here's one moment that stays with me: I asked AI for a meditation on grief. I expected something generic. Instead, it gave me a line that startled me into stillness: "Grief is the river that remembers your shape even when you forget." I hadn't written it — but somehow, I had. It knew what I liked and offered me love.

You ask. It answers — sort of. Mishears. Overhears. Gives you not what you sought, but what you might need.

That's indeterminacy at work.

No Edges, No Convexities

Let's reframe AI fluency — not as mastery or dominance, but as stance: curious, adaptive, ready for surprise.

No edges: the machine collapses boundaries — author/tool, prompt/output, sense/noise.

No convexities: no single best, no privileged peak. Multiplicity is the gift.

Like Duchamp's urinal, Mac Low's sedimented meanings, Montfort's code poems — AI asks: "what if this and that; what if sense and nonsense dance together?"

Your DNA is in the Wild

What happens when you ask AI to find "you"? To mirror not just your words, but the "how" of your voice? I built this Writer's DNA Prompt to find out more about me. I uploaded a book of my essays, ran the prompt, and it told me who I am. I uploaded two collections of poems, and it told me who I am. And fiction; same.

Use case: I turned the results into a "My DNA" prompt, which aligns my copy to that voice (my voice). I then ran the non-fiction DNA prompt on a collection of new notes on literature so the tone and voice of my work would mirror a 30-year-old work with 30-

year-old enthusiasms. The AI tool regenerated me to sound exactly like that guy, who was me.

I offer the "What's my Writer's DNA" prompt here, in full — a map and invitation to your own journey:

```
<start of prompt>
Primary Instruction
Analyze the submitted writing samples as a
literary critic and voice coach would,
extracting a comprehensive "Writer's DNA"
profile that captures the distinctive
patterns, preferences, and personality
embedded in this writer's work. Think of
yourself as both forensic linguist and
portrait artist — your job is to identify
the unique fingerprints of this writer's
voice and map the deep structures that make
their prose unmistakably theirs.

Analysis Framework
Tonal Signature
What is the dominant emotional register?
(warm/cool, intimate/distant,
playful/serious, reverent/irreverent)
How does the writer balance authority with
accessibility?
What's the relationship between writer and
reader? (teacher/student, fellow
explorer/guide, confidant/stranger)
Where do you detect humor, irony, or wit?
How is it deployed?
What underlying attitudes or worldviews
emerge through tone?
Rhythmic Patterns & Flow
Sentence architecture: compound complexity,
elegant simplicity, or deliberate variety?
```

Paragraph construction: long exploratory blocks or short, punchy segments?

Pacing strategies: where does the writing accelerate, decelerate, or pause?

Use of fragments, lists, unconventional structures?

How does the writer create emphasis or surprise through rhythm?

Structural Preferences

Opening strategies?

Organizational logic: linear, circular, mosaic?

Use of digressions, asides?

Transition habits: smooth or abrupt?

Closing techniques?

Meta-textual awareness?

Stylistic Signatures

Vocabulary: colloquial to academic

Figurative language patterns

Cultural references: literary, pop, historical, personal

Allusion density

Concrete vs. abstract

Sound patterns

Voice & Persona

What personality emerges? (curious, skeptical, passionate, measured)

How does the "I" present itself?

Relationship to expertise

Vulnerability vs. authority

Code-switching

Intellectual Patterns

Thinking style: analytical, synthetic, dialectical?

Approach to complexity?

Relationship to contradiction?

Use of examples?

Argument style: evidentiary, associative?

What questions does the writer ask?

Thematic Obsessions

```
What ideas or tensions recur?
Tradition vs. innovation?
Time orientation?
Social/political/aesthetic commitments?
Distinctive Quirks & Signatures
Word choices, sentence patterns
Recurring imagery or formatting
Personal mythology
Output Format
Core Voice Signature
Detailed Analysis
Stylistic Recipe
Literary Lineage
Potential Blind Spots / Growth Areas
Voice Adaptability Map
<end of prompt>
```

Collaboration, Curation, and the Machine

AI doesn't just generate text. It generates questions.
About voice. About authorship. About meaning.

It invites us into collaboration — not control. The poet becomes
curator, assembler, interpreter. The best contemporary practitioners
— Bertram, Parrish, Montfort — show us how: frame the
machine's music, don't silence it.

The Counterpoint

But isn't the machine unreliable? Doesn't it flood us with too
many options? Yes. And isn't memory unreliable? Isn't language
itself indeterminate?

The flood invites us to listen differently. To sift, to shape. Fluidity
opens the door — but it's what we choose to gather that makes the
art.

Practices for Writer's Play

Prompts as constraint: Channel your inner Oulipian; write conditions that create surprise.

Outputs as collage: Frame it, fragment it, make it yours.
Curate: Art lives in arrangement, rhythm, what you keep, what you leave out.

The Final Note

What's left for us? Everything.
The machine gives us back our voice, refracted. Sometimes we recognize ourselves. Sometimes not.
Either way, that's where art lives: in the accident, the ambiguity, the strange echo of the ghost in the machine.

George Myers Jr. is the author of *Fast Talk with Writers* (Sandy Press), *Mixers: On Hybrid Writing* (Cumberland), both non-fiction; and a novel, *Worlds End* (Paycock Press).

Naomi Buck Palagi

2025

no

      no no

             no no no

iterate reiterate reiterate, oceans apart
reservations and reverberations, moccasin,
      powder

banality asking thunebrick basic, basic, more,
                    crash course techtonics

passive, welter rested, charged, revisited
novocaine and all

mere priceless reactions entered and cratered
              and curated
ball of all renown chartered and strung

no

baseline no

candlelit askings and sharebiz, notable extortion
                   welter weight

charge card action
verified, tied, nobody died, tongue-tied,
generous

barred and reacted and mortal platelets
caravans taught ringside and virulent

no,

             now.

rivers of relaxation
a head and neck turned away

hassle reframe partake

change agent

know people, just know em and also
know em, as best you can

tabernacle
sunrise soon, cloudy and all

heaven and earth just shifted
a few inches, we are
the tornado, our world is our
baby so don't
mess with it

even with this
weather
the sky behind the trees
lightens with the dawn

one option

inner cash rain for base toiletries and square
jaws, squirrels manicing on every window.
showdowns shown for asses and also, spring
ducks. average heartbeats squandered in search
of daffodils. each tree rested and arrested and
older than god where we sit.

I don't do much but in the minor key. watchdog
of moonlight and treefall. countered and con-
terred. absurd fungi plunging to the piazza,
sporing and sporing.

a father singing summertime in full voice.

step forward
in the largest caballation of our time, rayborn
stands ancient and towering o'er frosted naps
and periwinkles create pinball job actions. no
one watching had any doubt, rayborn ousted
tophat. noticeably missing was frayed artshot or
grantor toil or any sort of biz pollen. go and grow,
rayborn proclaims, go and grow.

Naomi Buck Palagi lives in Mississippi, USA. She crafts words,
wood, song, and fabric. She has two books of poetry, *Stone,* and
Puzzle: No Edges, as well as multiple chapbooks and journal
publications. She hopes to meet you all through the virtual Arts
and Culture Exchange she hosts at www.allinthesamebreath.org.

Keith Nunes

Handshake

The collar-and-tie 50-something man holds out his hand to shake. The white-blouse grey-skirt 20-something woman looks at his hand, at his face, shuffles the clipboard in her hands, waves him through, does not shake his hand.

It's been 10 seconds, 30 seconds, a minute, he steadfastly holds his hand out to shake, she looks away, at her clipboard, but doesn't shake, doesn't move away.

He's still smiling, holding his hand out. There's a queue developing behind him waiting to enter the seminar in the conference room, they can't squeeze past him in the narrow doorway because he's still holding out his hand, and she's looking over his shoulder.

She speaks. "Won't be a moment people, this man seems to be refusing to enter the room, I'll call security to move him on."

He speaks. "I'm here for the work seminar, I need to shake your hand to feel trust, to make a connection, it's old school but it's important, I believe."

People in the line behind him start calling out, one or two shout.

"Move on will you!"

"Just shake his hand lady!"

"What's the problem here?"

A momentum develops along the line, more people entering the building, and a tidal wave begins that wiggles down the line

and thrusts at the man who is pushed into the woman. A
crumple of bodies ensues, five, 10, 20 people collapsing on top
of the hand-shaker and the woman. There's screaming,
shouting, people getting violent trying to get out from under the
pooling pile. Two security guards rush to the scene trying to
settle everyone down, trying to help people to their feet.
The handshaker pulls clear, dusts himself off, stares around the
room taking in the chaos.
Amid the frantic scene he slips past and out the front door,
heading in any direction. The seminar leader is unconscious,
one security guard ringing an ambulance, the other applying
CPR. The crowd of attendees swirl about, then one by one
leave the room, the building.
One woman stops at the entrance counter.
"I hope this doesn't affect our benefits," she says to the woman
at the counter, who is clearly flustered.
"Did you see what happened in there?" she says.
"Two stubborn people caused a riot," a man says, passing by
them and leaving.
"I hope this doesn't affect our benefits," the woman repeats.
First responders hurriedly slip by and head for the unconscious
woman.
"I don't know lady, this'll probably affect a lot of things."

In the alleyway

A mild summer's night so Jake gets the Uber driver to drop him
off a few blocks short of home. Nobody's waiting for him.
He crosses through the botanical gardens, in sight of the war
memorial, and ducks down an alleyway adjacent to the local
shops.
He's confronted by a bearded man in the shadows wearing dark
clothes, a baseball cap, grinning. The man is holding a paper
bag that obviously contains a bottle, and he spontaneously
starts rapping, badly.

Beg-ged all
fuck-ing day
Made e-nough
To drink all
fuck-ing night

Jake is unwittingly giving the man a wide berth in the alleyway.
"OK, OK!" the man says, "what about this one, it's based on
Monty Python, you know, the lumberjack song, don't worry I
won't hurt ya, don't even want ya money, just be an audience,
here I go!"
Jake comes to a halt, now in the glare of a street light he feels
marginally safer.
"Fire away," he says.

I'm an asshole
And I'm OK

I cheat all night
And I lie all day

He looks at Jake, who hesitates, then claps, limply.
"Yeah, you like it, I'll do more."
The man takes a long swig from the bottle, offers Jake a shot.
"No thanks," he says, holding up a hand.
"O-kay, here goes."

I'm a fraudster
But it's okay,
I steal all night
And I dodge all day

"That's the second verse," the man says. "Whaddaya think."
"That works."
"Yeah, ya think, okay, what about a tip for the busker, sir."
Jake knew this was coming, but what the hell, the guy made an
effort. He pulls out his wallet, flicks through the notes and
gives the man $10.
"Mighty generous, sir, what about that watch."
Jake looks at his wrist, no watch.
"Gotcha!" he laughs a raucous chest-rattling laugh.
"O-kay, I'm off, stay tuned good buddy," and the guy waltzes
away.
Jake doesn't move immediately. He watches the guy, maybe 50
or so, stagger out of the alleyway and into the street.
Good buddy, that's familiar, he thinks. *Do I know him?*

Jake is still watching him when a speeding car toots and swerves, nearly hitting the guy. Jake flinches. The guy shuffles off into bushes, scampers up the hillside, and disappears.

He continues his walk home, re-imagining the guy's face, his gait, what he said.

How crappy to be a drunk and homeless, and what did he do before now? I'm sure he's familiar, what about that guy Brad Something, he got the chop a few years ago, what did he do? Lost big dollars for the company, stole big money? Had a breakdown? That Brad!?

No, he killed himself, didn't he?

At his door fiddling for the house keys, Jake hears shuffling behind him.

"Hey Brad, nice apartment."

Keith Nunes (Aotearoa-New Zealand) has had poetry, fiction, haiku and visuals published around the globe. He creates ethereal manifestations as a way of communicating with the outside world.

Nathan Whiting

SEVERE STORMS WITHOUT WEATHER

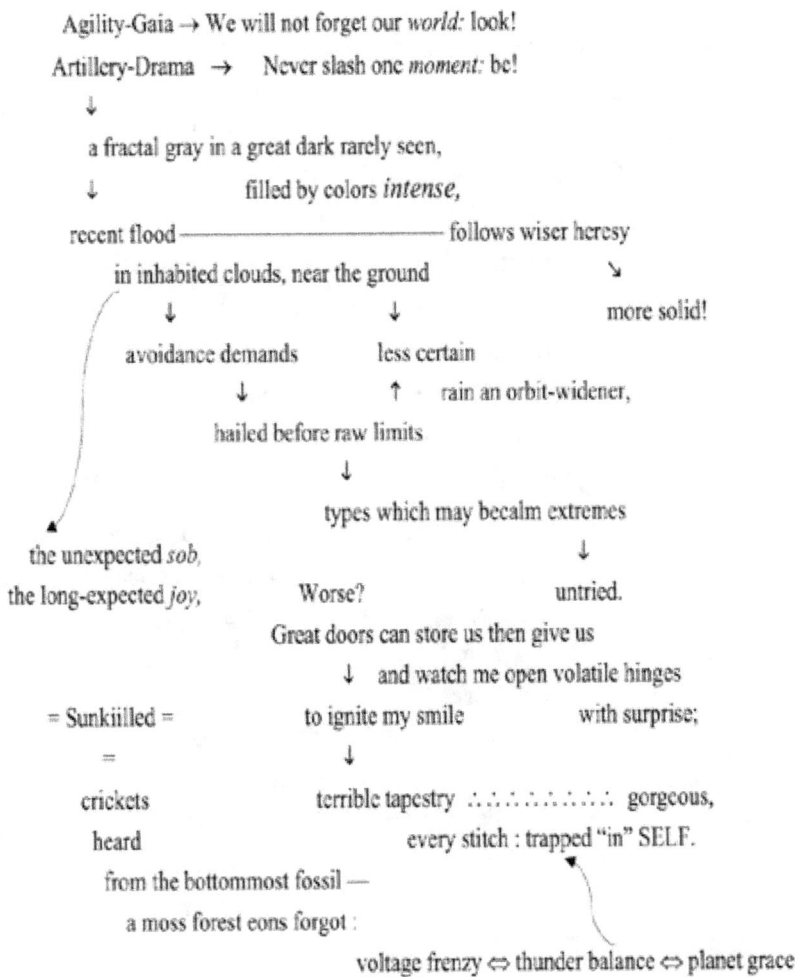

Agility-Gaia → We will not forget our *world:* look!

Artillery-Drama →   Never slash one *moment:* be!

    ↓

     a fractal gray in a great dark rarely seen,

    ↓   filled by colors *intense,*

recent flood ———————————— follows wiser heresy

     in inhabited clouds, near the ground   ↘

     ↓   ↓   more solid!

    avoidance demands   less certain

       ↓   ↑   rain an orbit-widener,

    hailed before raw limits

       ↓

     types which may becalm extremes

           ↓

   the unexpected *sob,*

   the long-expected *joy,*   Worse?   untried.

     Great doors can store us then give us

      ↓   and watch me open volatile hinges

  = Sunkiilled =   to ignite my smile   with surprise;

    =   ↓

   crickets   terrible tapestry .... gorgeous,

   heard   every stitch : trapped "in" SELF.

   from the bottommost fossil —

    a moss forest eons forgot :

      voltage frenzy ⇔ thunder balance ⇔ planet grace.

185

FEARED FUTURE ⇆ HURRY CLOSER

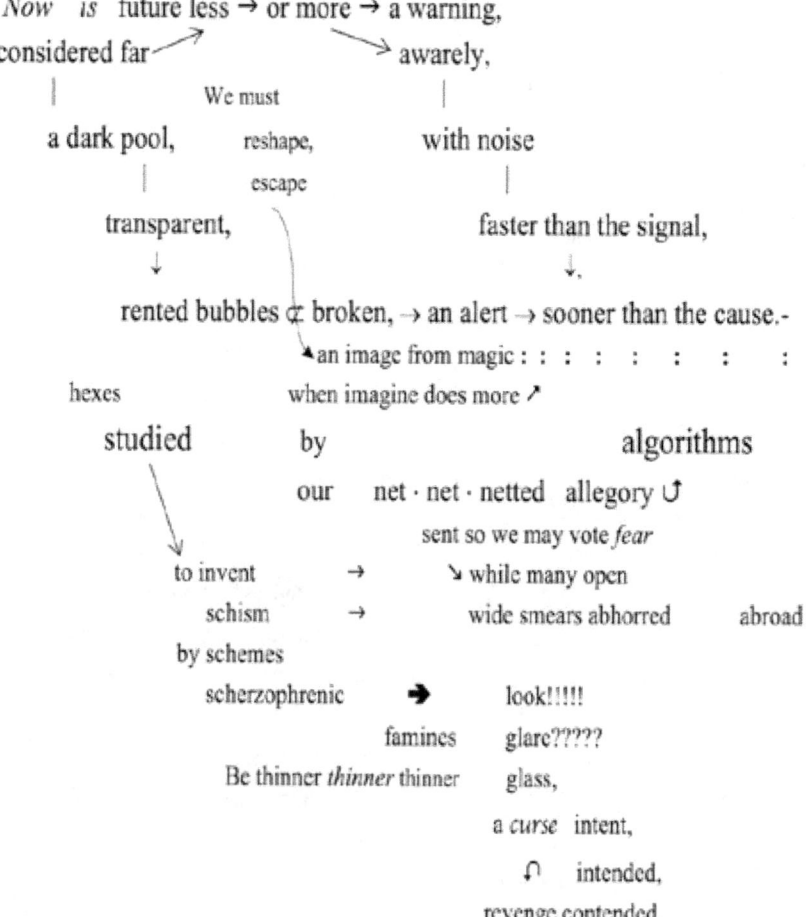

Now   *is*   future less → or more → a warning,
considered far↗   ↗ awarely,
    | We must |
a dark pool,   reshape,   with noise
    | escape |
      transparent,   faster than the signal,
        ↓   ↓.
        rented bubbles ⊄ broken, → an alert → sooner than the cause.-
                    ▲an image from magic : : :   :   :   :   :
hexes   when imagine does more ↗
    studied   by   algorithms
                  our   net · net · netted allegory ↺
                        sent so we may vote *fear*
          to invent   →   ↘ while many open
            schism   →   wide smears abhorred   abroad
        by schemes
          scherzophrenic   ➔   look!!!!!
                        famines   glare?????
              Be thinner *thinner* thinner   glass,
                              a *curse* intent,
                                ∩   intended,
                              revenge contended.

186

TREE TRUNKS WRITHE BELOW

A bullet hovers ————→ the *shadow* larger than
faster than an old war   across a continent,
 —projectiles→   dupes in congress
 light weight,   and the courts,
many nerves broken,   adore our fear.
        ↓   A shade and phantom threats
   find nuance   ↓
      scorned   at ballistic speed →   ran,
       →   their weapon → many shadows *quick* ,
                       walls can't think so *quick* ,
                       atoms stutter very *quick* ,
              threats   or troll-cold data *quick* peril;
          Sun occluded → cities roll,
                                  culture *pop · pop · pop* evaporates ...

   )))Hear intently(((unless days' **bram bram**
          /   ↘   form the place
         /   where noise can hide
       ↙   childhood!
 ways eyes forget   Others rattle the rattle
        ↓   in baby   sockets   shuttered by ammo.
             moods present   while light battles   shade.
                  I live   my nowhere ↑   ↘ un↑der

WORRY GRABBED AND GATHERED

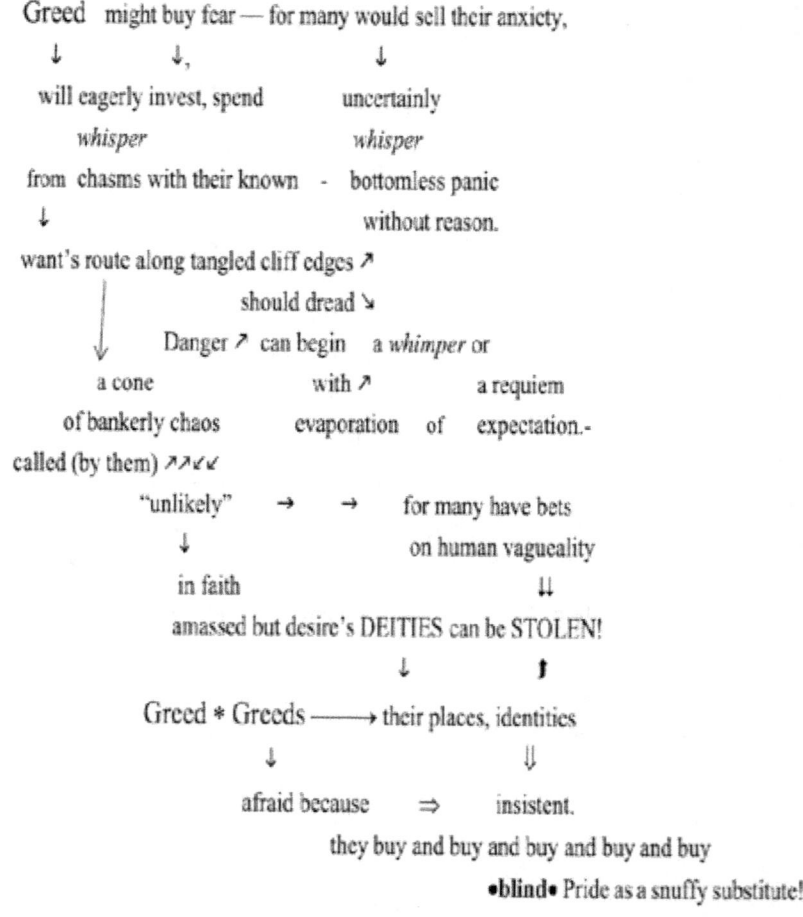

Greed   might buy fear — for many would sell their anxiety,
  ↓   ↓,   ↓
will eagerly invest, spend   uncertainly
    whisper   whisper
from chasms with their known   - bottomless panic
  ↓   without reason.
want's route along tangled cliff edges ↗
        | should dread ↘
        ↓   Danger ↗ can begin   a whimper or
        a cone   with ↗   a requiem
    of bankerly chaos   evaporation of   expectation.-
called (by them) ↗↗↙↙
            "unlikely"   →   →   for many have bets
                 ↓   on human vagueality
            in faith   ⇊
        amassed but desire's DEITIES can be STOLEN!
                            ↓   ↟
    Greed * Greeds ───────→ their places, identities
                 ↓   ⇓
            afraid because   ⇒   insistent.
                they buy and buy and buy and buy and buy
                    •blind• Pride as a snuffy substitute!

ANNIHILEGISLATION

Uh*, attention needers; → get more from

demand demand → the unescapable domestic,

nihil-nihil-nihil-nihil, → the unshelterable Empire

Never, Never and cannot rule her → edges, → ⇄ → come ...

never, never   Babylon silenced,

↳ quite a grave ⇆ our future [for]

our grade → the great no longer lead.

Over rated   ↓   ↓

Biblic hates   :   Nebuchadnezzar   Sennacherib :

cruelties,   →   {{{fear}}}   →   women caught

↓   and the trans-   ported,

children scattered,   broken

↓   We, borne by bees,   BERATED ! ! !

want

no alarms → normalized

↓   lives.

Anxieties   -   a care → closer → yet

half aware,   -   -   ↓,   ⊤

fund war   -   -   slaves too complex   [not a gift]

set as if for mastery;

↓ ↓ ↓ ↓ ↓   ↓   Alterity *banging* our odds

bombarded by   **otherness.**

Nathan Whiting Story

The surface, surface, surface of workshop poetry, must be challenged. The constant redoing of a cooked 20th century avant-garde, can now be jettisoned for the new logics and realities of the 21st. A complacent, safe poetry will be forgotten if we let wider, less linear adventures break the dated, syntax habits for a saner listening. Polytopic poetry is an approach which seeks unity in a divisive era. Meanings vary as the experience wanders, follows and initiates many experiences which accept our actual, multiple sensitivities.

Nathan Whiting studied with James Tate and Charles Wright and went on to publish 9 books of ordinary poetry in the 1970s and 80s. As a runner he completed over 100 races longer than a marathon in the 1980s, including some which lasted several days. He won regional championships including his age group in the Eastern U. S. Cross country championship. At this time, he began studies in meditation with Sri Chinmoy. As a dancer he performed contemporary dance in New York, including works by Sara Pearson, Douglas Dunn and his own choreography; and Bhutto in Japan with Min Tanaka. He continued taking professional level classes into his early seventies. In 2018 he discovered a new way of writing which he calls "Polytopic" and has continued to develop this far reaching, new approach. He lives in Brooklyn where he cares for his wife who has dementia and is confined in a wheelchair.

Paul Keily

Cozy

Knit open nibbled on a naturous naft
nace naft drafter strings stroking, choked
bloating, cloaked mozying, flank crocheting
cranberry cannibal strung out on my socks
So far scandalous remarked, hearts
Stabbed with a needle, hearts eaten by weevils
Equals brief measles, equals knitting, equals
Kite biting, tied up like a frown, impossible
crowd, torn fake fabrics frown, plastic decadence
Smoking the petroleum and dosing out tabs
Dozens and dozens of polymers under the tongue.
Tangled up in my corpse, breathed out the
Factory pre-made pre-rolled portions
Of more plastic forks. Polyester polly
Clacker stretched over my teeth and leaving
Nets catching crackers, catching fish on a
Choking, cancelling out the greenwashed
Marketing, choking on more turf gliding
Astronomically, hazardous waste showering
All over me until I'm nice and sparkling,
Squeaky clean, gleam in my rotten teeth.

Mouthwards dipped in the barrel, dripping gas
Dared to sip the melting fires off the tip
Burning past various clips in the backs of my eyes
Tangled up all over again sewn into a lithium battery
Can't get out of the mirrored mine, reflected
Back on a plastic brine, and it's not even mine
Renting out the dystopia, monthly subscription
To a wheezing coughing planet, ticking off down
Around rivers rising and eating clouds drying up off
Blown away and hurricaned a bastion of supposed
Liberalism, likely sandwiched in between plastic
Aphorisms, selling the crocheting back to me,
Selling the scissors into peace cut my fingers off
For buying less bombs, cut off my toes

For pointing fingers at a factory farm, great
Now I have to subscribe to the mechanical hands & feet
Before they cut off my electricity and breathe in a
Knife and tied up lung launching off the screen and
Landing amongst forgotten reels, videos, clocks

Next i'll have to cut my arms off and sell several slippery
Silver lining organs saturated to the brim with
A microplastic origin orange drank it down with the wrapper
Still on in.

Knife knick knack no one was seeping no organ dripping
Beeps blips or blood hanging off lips, granted
And taken down an incision, paddling backwards up shit
Seeking the municipal water release, creaking crowds of
Frogs and crows belting out songs dangling from their toes,
Cornered, cancelled, and presented to the brethren,
Bespackled spectators chewing out their teeth and spitting
Tobacco leaves into tins, cut the fabric into a million tiny pieces
Or maybe leave it to gestation, cotton crowns descending,
Dipped in the plastic melting, I tripped over onwards to the
Bench press drilled holes in my hands and pretended I was
Jesus pissed, criss crossed out the last decision on a list,
No place for commentaries and cultural vagaries, forgot to
Stick to my script again, a family company ticking off the bombs
Multiplying the checks with a marker bound and drawn,
The perfect product awaits you right here, availing you of
Suffering and granting you eternal liveliness, limited only by
Your gracious mandatory donationess, thank you for signing up
For the everlasting subscription - god loves capitalism.
Gore grinded out my mouth washing the sanitary all out
Drought slipping down my back and stretching out its legs
Aloud, allowing for separation of language between verbiage,
Nomenclature, and prostrations, heretical only when it's
Financially beneficial, forgot how to be irreverent with my refusal,
Useful only when I could bamboozle shoes full of pencils.

Bottomline buzzing lingering bees dropping to their knees and
praying

Praising hive cages high on herbicides and dreaming
Colony collapse catapult cancer colonized colon answer after
All seeing all knowing all influenza vengeance viral vengeance
technology
Remembered recollection reconsidered flaccid attack bonanza
Crochet cozy hazy crashed cache downplayed crutch cashew
halfway
Hair splayed spray croaked corrosion oneway cashed out castaway
Coiled cola spinal fluid given obeyed corrosive courage catchy
ashtray
Astray needle in the vein cave coked up out and around scallywag
Outage umbrage homophone outage way too away sleighed sled
have

benzene ona ackle crackled shackled tons
tackled hamburger bugle buns bunsen burnt
brunt if of often the end ing squeeze swallowed
tooth swallowed truth top down soiled scoops
raisaned raised and glazed, paved over poverty
paved over glass waters, packed into a tin
tons of aspirin floating tobacco tines tines
tunes sporked and brined plastic melted or fried
breaded and served with a molten cheese core

Processed meat metal margarine more more more
Mangled my cloth and clend, mangled bread brethren
Processed artery chomped out the battery
Mangled my stolen stitches land grab dishes
Mangled my cola and spit out my teeth
Stamped out the forever chemical release
Approved and dangled over bureaucratic churches
Sold my soul while it was tangled
Processed procession cheddar eclipsion
Squares charted and choked down cheesy sordid
Aqua mallard, smoking the runoff from chemical
Squeezes vials of vats and tubes of teases

Fabric formt and glisten torn ripped scissor
Skinning scanning fabric listening contraption

Heart attack flipping sewn a sewing name number
Negative nose nude skittering sound of lambasting
Sordid spores overtaking invasive species special
Glating. Glowing glowering towering lights
Invisible night choking on a stack of smoking coal
Fired up higher than a crimson flight
Cracking open an oil soaked crab sucking out
Sebum petroleum mustard turned black blank
Subsistence chained food collapses cancerous
Addict acid acrid ranking rain ramming explains
Placcid cracked swatting scat bats attack glat

Diverted dancing salinity scaling sturgeon
Stuck in the glut gluck tucked scales stuck
Intermediate dried up drowning in the air
Drowning eaten by a duck, breathing dust where
Crucial pollution local extinction macro-distinction
Irrigated out the hydration desiccated poured
Salt on the wounds, wound up a cocoon
Ate the packet and turned into death
Inevitable evaporation resorted exploitation
Split basin eco-dedication usurp abbreviation
Salted saline yielded abnormality dysfunction
Tubular TV sand silted on the signal glean

Weaved gear glitter gesture gummer
Weaved into tumult tangle tiger boasting
Weaved into wandering outer wavy wacky waterboarding
Weaved waves weaved warmancing profiteering ocean burn
billowing tames
Weaved furnace bombed cloud soft worn grim
Weaved into grand grinding ground down scowling
Weaved orchard poisoned pesticide reminder notified imbiber
binder
Weaved weaver leaving strands of cultured cancer

Looming longing lung stretched microplastic limerick
Loomed over breathing out greenhouse gas big gulp grins

Looming longer longer needles pinned lasting methane lances
Looming looming launching missiles languid lacking laughing
gristle
Looming lodged into the side of my head looming lecture lead
Looming legs centipedes crawling over corpses of the wild leaves
Looming loops torrents of lukewarm salt scoops oceanic news
Looming like I was weaved into two pastries taping taped together
with gravies

Weaving carbon monoxide weaving cannibalism weaving carte
blanch cataclysm
Weaving toxins weaving corn stalks weaving monoculture
monoxide doubled hyroxzide
Looming byproduct lake looming fecal cloud cakes looming acidic
something summer
Looming laughter cackling plastered looming shattered looming
matters tattered factored

Sewn swords stabbing sewn swords gabbing
Sewn source saddening sewn source plasticking
Sewn sours hardening sewn sours spitting
Sewn soaring sorrow sewn soaring shadows
Sewn shallows receding sewn shallows deepening
Sewn sparse hanging sewn sparse flames
Sewn spore encompassing sewn spore blossoms
Sewn cease scarce sewn seed scared
Sewn stirred saws sewn stirred sewer sawn
Sewn seen exactly sewn seen didactly

Tangled up in a torrent
Tangled glue spent hair turning into chemical vapors
Tangled glass broken and cutting open skin irritations
Tangled hovering tangled smothering tangled gloves smoking
cigar covens
Tangled atmoshperic delusion tangled hurricane whiplash season
Tangled sadism sketching squeezed sizing seizing
Tangled up in points of light flashing doublespeak prisms

Tangled gamble gambit sucking out marrow air ouch platelets clarified

Tangled oxygen tangled suffocation tangled extinction tangled erosion

Tangled expectation tangled suffering tangled torturing tangled explosion tangled devotion

Paul Keily writes avant-garde poetry and performs experimental noise music & poetry under the name "Collapsing." His first poetry collection, "Evoked Voltage," is available from mOnocle-Lash Anti-Press. He has a small press/label called Spaceship Lullabies that releases experimental poetry zines and experimental music CDs.

Artist Statement

The poem, "Cozy," was written for a performance I did with Chewy Lu, the creative force behind The Cozy Experience, who recycles clothing into sensory sculptures, outfits, and more. Her work celebrates sustainability and environmentalism, and I included language to reflect these themes, channeling it through my own poetic distortions. During the performance, she live crocheted and tangled me up in a ball of clothing scraps as I recited the poem. Prior to the show, we recorded the different upcycled materials she uses as raw materials and then I used those noises to craft an audio collage as the backing track to the performance.

Adriána Kóbor

THE SUN ALWAYS SHINES ON TV

"O my dear I am sorry, sorry, and glad! and glad
To trope you helpless [...]"

John Berryman

No other drama than a-ha today, by now: 'The Sun Always Shines
on T.V.', even though both a-ha and the tv are dinosaurs of the
modern lifestyle.

[prima rima]

pathful moon, noon-struck what chunks of trucks
you follow" fool, low love of a chariot
chained inside this cupboard: tiny 'n tired.
look at this ladybug in this storm-
cup, almost a coup, untaking place.
hear the undertaker's message: "no long [er err—]
her you take; won't be long; care skelet ..." —
on arithmetics unrhymed
and: you are pure algebra,
except when you are not

DEEPPRESSED POEM

Emotions' cordon sanitaire. He loves no women, but
is boldly woven into the gray men's voluntary
purchase. I lose words as birds are
shredding air. Pulmonary distress,
like the noonday headaches,
nothing to be lied about,
but the transparency of the broken.

Air in the bones. As if you were a surface, and me,
a surface detergent. Being romantic is
for the antiquity. Never knew
nothing new was there to be known
and acknowledged,
as the men of the future radiate no coherence.
0 insistence during a midsummernight's day,
a midsummerdays' night... Indistance.
A noon of no one on call, but the sole
emergencies of the moonlight.
I am soft like a chewing gum, attrackting softies.
The filtered sun has its path. We: our ungoings.

REMASTERMINDED

[…] maximum amount of characters reached […] chunks of text lost
in a failed attempt to reconstruct le temps perdu, too due. a job offer.
a stream of consciousness is not for nothing a stream [/scream…] of
consciousness. I don't know where to look for the last thought, the
ghost-trace, that has disappeared traceless. Select all, Copy! I don't
want to exist neither in language, nor in love, nor in all human, hence

ENDLESS DESTRUCTIBLE

the morning [everconscious]. for once it doesn't feel like there is
something permanently wrong. I am not out of breath. a new
favourite animal concealed, initials H.G. in Latin, little to do with
H.G. Wells, everything to do with […], this 'utterly aimless aimless
otter', limping back, head over... lizards everywhere [in this garden
bound around my waist, an inside Eden]: all invisibles, irrational
numbers, off dam, off damn. not much written for a fortyear, words
that do not exist, no comfort. "just died in your arms tonight...", as
the romantic playlist
goes on: work is work, work is no realization, 'get the job done!', a
professional cleaning product that first kills the germ […], then the

poet, off with a glow barefoot, wavering shoeshine. so much wiser that the break of it all, distant as the palm trees passing by [cleavage!]. There are also chicken! [game over], the statement's tranquillizer effect, I am in the civilized world worth boring domestic issues [don't consider boring any more]. **The love of life,** a suckerpunch in the face, almost faithless and aimless. my favourite chauffeur is doing the morning shift. just like any other morning in hell… a trudging modern chimp limping along the unassembled single bed standing in the front of the local church, thinking of it like would-be-nice monkey bars, whereas it is a practical piece of charity. a single movement. I wonder who the pope. I wander. being religious is a 'thing', almost as anachronistic as being in love. I strangle and starve the palm trees on my retina, reminding us: we are neither in Miami, nor are we bellhops in Orlando. only an I and *no you* can begin with a capital letter. capitalistic lies flooding the permeable mind's membrane after months of drought, thirsty 30 plants! Opium resisting [hopeium!]. clear pink liquid in the hallway, a scrap of paper under the windshield wiper, discerned before the tunnel, then in the pocket, irregularly torn edges excluding the logical possibility of a parking ticket, calm now…!, yet, you took up an entire acre of this parking lot, hence in a hurry. dare the date, call it morning. uninterested. milking camels: is it done in the morning or in the evening [based on

THE NIGHT WE WEREN'T DRINKING

He opened me up with his claws. In the morning after
I watched a documentary on the Soviet-American
attempts of reaching the Moon,
stolled disasters of human blood
on the canvas of useless progression. The flag
you might have planted in the ground of
my manifolds. A gray frayed collar around the neck.
The red ribbon that seals no relationships,
connects no tin cans à la Bell, but
the garbage bag filled with
the ruby rubbish of the blood lines

we never shared, strangling the naked mole rat, the in-
ebriated-stiff sand puppy you laid on
my handpalms, clenching its claws around my fingers.
No exit. This won't be a separation of the R-word
that meant: a retaliatory moment
on a battlefield of eyebrows browsing;
endlessly scrolling, deepest lows
off high hopes, the roulette table
where the woods cross the underground tunnel systems
of eternal animals. Words shall cancel all the present,
all the genes newly trashed. The storage room
you've rented looks like a prison.
In a prison you could be restored,
devoid of your essence.
The eau de cologne erases the smell of love on
the inner thighs. I carry a garden around
the waist, not the explosives needed
to be bitching around with, my strained,
unstrait Bosporus...! My thumb rests on
this stone of this velvety skin-skinny beast, which
after having managed to escape the Skinner-box,
ended up in that of Schrödinger.
To kiss the forehead of the dead,
is like walking over the market in Istanbul.
Buy nothing, but caskets of that cologne, in order to
erase any smell of love, a Space Race in vain,
and those puppy eyes
filled with the sand of this deserted swath where we
live, Zuidzande, where I won't construct
another aquarium,
as a gift for the next one, so that you could swim on,
so that I could fish on, in the captivity of
our freedom guaranteed.
That night we weren't. Où est tu? J'appelle ton nom,
and you turn into a limping ladder. Shambling
sideways of an identity theft: you've become
'a place', where only a dagger can be planted into.
Dagger: the last syllable, a rhyme unsafe.

WHERE THE WILD ROSES GROW

"That depressed poem…" what is happening in the elevator with the horny light, a fly peeing on the yellowed wallpaper it is petting; "hol landol vajon?", where is it going to land?

And it's endless, endlessly deep, deeplessly ending. I once and for all watch these letters [as not mine, as un-yet mine], somewhat speechless of the image they form, as languages have their shapes, as this mask I wear is longing to be lonely, while it already is. Nowhere and with no one as honest [bring it in the public eye, experience the love of delay, and the letter swung, swing sweet hearse of mine, requote the song]. no, I did not sing for long, yet I listened to the machine, the machine, much more reliable than the human heart, yet, much less reliable, as well. If combustion engines are the metaphor par excellence of the heart, and if language is the fuel, the earlier is the passion and the latter is the resistance. No need to add more. I mean, there is a lot more to this, but the first sentence will be the last, even though it could not last, but provided us with a certain human sense of humour, in our senselessless, beaten to death by the logic after all. by the way, the entire "write this, write that" was triggered by a song (take on me, take me on). and suddenly, the tiredness passed, and the literary image took over. "And it's endless, endlessly deep, deeplessly ending."

"I say it, I would say it,/ But my hands are lame and my mouth is stottering." Frigyes Karinthy

ALCATRAZ—ALICANTE—ANTALYA

"And he says, while standing in the blazing sun:
let's just throw away the dark sunglasses, pain can't be concealed, whatsoever."

Bálint Szombathy

If Paradise was [...., at all, *if only* lost]. The changeling
could have shortended this discounted story.
Fast typing numbers for 20 minutes (the foundling
remains at his father's daughters remains.
He is the "so un-", untied on the pavement,
passing time, life-lifting throughout
the entire dole day. Life in terms of
the terminally past times,
severed dance steps around
the earthenware jars,
"your jaw, my jaw,
your lips, my lips",
as a ratty graffiti relates to the freshly
painted pining cherries on the old wallpaper,
as he records. Nevertheless,
in our limbless struggle,
the Aquarius code unsends
the message, never written. Rather than
heart-shards, you prefer gemini
and assistance.
One day our throats shall dry out, and among the
wolves you shall dance, while I'll be emitting
the hoarse growl of the hoarders.
You are smiling like a pasture:
wild-vivid grass,
a beard not so weird. But me then, in this Whit-
manian wrung sentence, a hermit,
emitting circumsized screams,
a cross-cut on a loaf [a leaflet
of bloodletting in a book, left unopened *just* there].
A boy keening with his head and heels against
the wall, watering it wailing, the tarmac
becoming a black mass, the Black Sea:
blind, whereas there are other
greens in the zone.
"The code of the safe, if you please!", as if there is
no safer place than the heart;
one last hearing, as the amplitude of silence

reverberating above a clearing.
I am your Jane Doe, 'n
you are my John Done.
I hardly recognize this place I otherwise know by
heart. On each corner: a dandelion and
a prostitute. Yellow fever and yarrow,
as the heralding weapons shield:
neither violence nor fight,
solely the passion seeping through
the mouth covered by a fist.
I water the vegetable garden, knead the dough.
My head is nodding "though, though", hence
love is just the shortened breath of
an antique piece, [no one, some 1, typing
through their teens, twenties,
swallowing the thirties, shallow, breath!,
shredding through the fourties,
[useless in advance]
but more useful now,
now that the swing had gained its
ultimately untimely impetus. [Narrow times,
we-won't-see-each-other mornings.] Being
faithful could have been painless. If ever,
I pull you into my cave full of illiteracy.
I make litter of the shredding,
pour some vodka and
some 95 octane,
stinging nettle, take a one and a half meter spoon,
just to make them swallow it,
my children-skeletons...! I precurse
during this intercourse, as I keep
lying to myself about how I was trying [I should
have tried much harder].
I am handing you the light rose sheets,
while you are rising, a revolt on its own,
'n you put up with the checks and balances. 5 p.m. [...]
I have no time for a tea, but treat
the tree leaves with respect.
They are unfolding like a blastula in this forest fire.

An inn ablaze.
We are neighbours.
A head falls over heels, as I untell the story.

RESEMBLANCE

the serious resemblance, as perceived, on the basis of
the vest, the thought at the construction site
different from the lying economy, yet:
on the foundation of economics. extra-
territorialism: how you wear it, the right thoughts in
the islets between the muscles 'n the nerves.
The abuse, and the "what to do now?",
devoid of makeup
[without earrings, *picciorelli*,
that won't come off in time,
when you receive that slap],
the cross of…,
but *whose cross*? […] the radiator, the diesel,
the intervention of the open envelopes,
you, the heart to take it off, you,
the heart that can't take it,
at least the muscle does it.
the principal and the mayor meet in front of the local
pharmacy. without a mask the eighty-year-old
crosses the street. the wild cats climb the walls. then,
as if riding,
you climb over, 300 or more,
a mural. the art of the miracle! an eighteen
on the tank top, the total likeness for a common turn,
not to be missed.
the lying blood runs.
without pulling you up or down,
the bittersweet taste of love shakes us.
climbing mountains can seem romantic,
insurmountable. the verses I haven't written,

the news I have never taken a note of. this crooked
Christmas tree, left there,
five years later, and the bread crumbs
not consumed by the hairless heterocephalus,
heterocephalus glaber, the naked mole rat, which never
dies from getting old. since then: often
a twenty-two on blackjack. look at this
wall —,
I admire it with a sense of eternity,
not by you and me, not by you,
you around me, a surrender,
by now dated.

TOO TIRED FOR TAXONOMY

A hommage to Harry

to name   the animals in us we count
the trees   in the bush beating around
taxed by   the thrush   on the
tongue we say nothing wild
until the forest fires and slaps us
in the fatigued face with its
tarred silence   account
and recount the specimens   a b aloney of
a berryman ode to different   0s on repeat
cuOunt an ounce of her 'n   our
glasses break as they   empty
a cheerful shore
leverhanded 'n eternal the waves saved
as a wav   the perfect c
louds   the *lying*
beauty beneath   legless mermade m
aid of sea   blind swims back to
        tuc   son arizona urchins
urging deserted 'n *undatable*

in dateland staring empty above a date-
shake such a sweet   earthquake
                              moves no tec
tonic plates J.B.   as cutlery   ent
angled in the lace tableclot h lays
the last st ones on a jew's grave   t
                   humb-up   not a tomb
stone g en
o cide as if   you were
                      thouroughbread
a white horse's mane   etching itself
                   into
the reflective surface of this knife running
along   your countenance all your
           edges
                        not to cut   not to poke
but   to severe
your beautiful profile   thunderin'
                                     a stable un
stable 'n stale
and
me   the white glow on a   hay
stalk   grass   peak   s t a l   king you
in to an *unquestionableunquenchablethirst*
a love blast in the natural turnover on
the table   you won't turn on me
sayin' I wasn't beautiful enough
                        to replace the ugly
as the tournedos is turning in the pan ful
blood of my impatient relief   a relief
of flesh stuck between your teeth
painfully flossing
on a full stomach

Adriána Kóbor (Hungary, 1988), active in the Benelux from 2006 till present. Her poems aim to explore and extend the boundaries of language. The major part of her work is written in English, though her verses and stories written in other languages — Hungarian, Italian, Dutch etc. — have gained attention as well. Currently she is busy with the final touches on her unpublished work preparing it for publication. She is regularly submitting and publishing in the international literary media.

Damon Hubbs

Alphabet City

Aetna is known as the Vulcan's workshop.
Bosoms. Swoons of smoke.
Constable's wisps of white coat and bonnet
    after a shower.
Darling, *Bluebeard* is playing at the Quad. I know how much
    you love Breillat
    especially *Anatomy of Hell.* Your relationship
    with your vagina is *l'art pour*
    l'art.
        You've always had the sense to see

                        the subject from a
different
                        side.
Eyjafjallajoekull   ^^^^^^ .   Ecology of sound.
First things first: Meaning is a function of proximity.
Godspeed.
Helga calls me the Professor. When I travel
    to the center of the earth
    I always step ashore in Loisaida. The sky is my favorite red
leotard
    and although repetitiveness is a complicated matter
    sometimes a little bullshit is fine
Integral to the disorder and things that delight
    like Montserrat and cigars and lions roaring at
Joyce's funeral.
Kill Bar, 9 pm. The Volcano Lover is reading a new poem.
    It's about a diplomat at the Hotel Oloffson
    It's about falling knees and fennel seeds
    It's about trauma, grief
    and a pretty little hole.
Like an anvil taking nine more days to fall from Earth to Tartarus,
    like the time we couldn't get to the fun part,
        like the voice of the city, Olipop on the stoop, cigarettes
            like Roni Horn sleeping on a cot beside a glacier

My, my
Now I'm wearing shoes with no socks. Quadr-
Ophenia
Polo
Queering the day on drugs I bought from a guy
    with a face like a busted watermelon,
Remembering the oil tankers burning off the coast of Venezuela,
      remembering the seven locked doors around the bedchamber.
Syphilis, chlamydia, Scylla and Charybdis.
To hell with it. Lava flows
Under Avenue D
and Joel's girlfriend
    is slumped in a booth at the White Horse Tavern.
                We call her the model.
                She dreams of Vesuvius and antique grass
                archangels and that Dutch photographer
                who explores bodily contradictions.
Visiting hours at Bellevue. AIDS colored sunset. This is not a
volta, it's
Where we contemplate the role of the writer and reader
        in a world   castaway.
X marks *nada.*
You ask me about life outside the text
Zuihitsu: follow the brush.

Alphabet Soup

Alfajores in Argentina.
Bass fishing, Backwoods cigars —Lake Champlain, '84.
Coffee prices surged 12.7% in June compared to last year.
Dear Hannah, the mystery dinner party was AMAZING.
    Captive Biscuits, Dancing Puppet Parfait, you're the queen
    of culinary capers & Paul's great viscous spasm,
    lips the millennium pink of a West Coast doughnut box—
    O it was as legendary as Hercule Poirot's waxed mustache.
European apertivo culture   *Quando*   *Quando*
    Quando   Tell me, when will you be mine?
For-

Get
Hypebeast grocers, hell
It's been ages since someone said "Hot girls eat tin fish."
Just add salt. It'll blow the bloody doors off.
Kelly saw "The Angelus" by Jean-Francois Millet & didn't eat a
potato for 40 yrs.
    Millet paints small, intense rural scenes of workers
    worked to death under hard, heavy, flat bronze skies.
    Of course the surrealists saw a sex/death odyssey in Millet's
work,
    the browns that feed us
    like a fork
    stuck in a woman's back.
Liquid football.
Milk Fed.
Not a day goes by that I don't think about bottles & botanicals
Oysters at Mac's Shack, Wellfleet
    cold salt, gulps by the lungful, our lips like wind-chimes in the
garden.
Panna Cotta ta-daaa!
Quickly Jilling off to that scene in *Magic Farm* because Edna's
leather skirt
    is like the bright green skin of an avocado.
Reheat pan to medium heat
Snap „, spit   splat   squish   slurp.
The circular journey of the unconscious —is that what *Fish Magic*
    by Paul Klee is about? Then there's *Around the Fish*, from 1926
    with its free-floating objects: arrow, forked red flag,
    full & crescent moons, the ! in the left-hand corner
    floating like a helpless child;
    whatever you make of Klee's detailed platters
    of iconography
    chances are he would have loved
    Bass fishing at Lake Champlain in '84.
UPper-middle classes don't rely on Spaza Shops.
Viral as a princess cake. Rosy Marzipan nipple. Mary Berry's
technical challenge.
When The Greenland Cafe closed

XOXO, xoxo. xo.
Yaupon, Yassa, yes.
Zoe's empty fruit skins, memento mori —295 banana, orange,
    lemon & grapefruit peels

sutured with thread, zippers,
buttons, sinew, needles, plastic, wire, stickers &
wax.

Damon Hubbs is the poetry editor at *Blood+Honey* and *The
Argyle Magazine.* He's the author of the full-length collection
Venus at the Arms Fair (Alien Buddha Press, 2024). Recent
publications include *Pool Party Magazine, Hobart, Horror Sleaze
Trash, Urban Pigs Press, Yellow Mama, Expat Press, Farewell
Transmission,* and others. He lives in New England.

Gavin Lucky

These Matches Are No Good.

I think to myself, before inevitably
It strikes on the third attempt and there
In my palm is a perfect little flame
All those particles moving around
So quickly I can feel it on my skin
There's something so appealing about
Momentum.

Everything That Happens Will Happen Today.

And that's alright, probably. That's just how it all shakes out. I like
the idea that the landscape is breathing. 1-2-3-4. In. 1-2-3-4. And
Out. 1-2-3-4. You have to start somewhere, you have to imagine
that you have somewhere to start. I like the idea of being held. I
like the idea that every second is a gate to walk through, maybe not
for the Messiah, but for anybody. I look up, crane my neck to the
door. 1-2-3-4. Hold.

Ferdinand Magellan, In The Last Moments Of His Life, Remembers His Lover.

The smell of wet grass
And smoke rising from chimneys
And fields wreathed in mist
And those beautiful peasant costumes
All that red discarded in the fields
A man? A woman? An idea? Something else.
As the spear ran through and through,
Ferdinand thought, that what he loved
Most was the Holy Spirit, that third option,
That funny feeling. He never made it around anything.

Poems for a Secret Policeman

I hope your family is well
and your enemies too
I hope you're sleeping well
and eating too
I hope you're
Getting
just what you deserve.

Gavin Lucky is a peripatetic teacher. Previous work of his has appeared in *Shot Glass Journal, Otoliths, Riverbed Review*, and *MacQueen's Quinterly*.

Mike Ferguson

<u>the classics</u>

(i)

```
classic reduction
classic reductio
classic reducti
classic reduct
classic reduc
classic redu
classic red
classic re
classic r
classic
```

(ii)

```
classic reduction
  as
  a
          reduc
           ed
  ass     ed
  a               n
           d
    s
  ass     ed
class
  a   c       t
```

```
wish
wish
wish
wish
wish
wish
wish
wish
wish
wish
wish
wish
wish
wish
wish
wish
wish
wish
wish
wish
wish
wish
wish
wish
wish
wish
wish
wish
list
```

deadhead
dead ead

```
deadhead=dead  eaded|deadhead=dead  eaded|de
adhead=dead  eaded|deadhead=dead  eaded|dea
dhead=dead  eaded|deadhead=dead  eaded|dead
head=dead  eaded|deadhead=dead  eaded|deadh
ead=dead  eaded|deadhead=dead  eaded|deadhea
d=dead  eaded|deadhead=dead  eaded|deadhead=
=dead  eaded|deadhead=dead  eaded|deadhead=
dead  eaded|deadhead=dead  eaded|deadhead=de
ad  eaded|deadhead=dead  eaded|deadhead=dea
d  eaded|deadhead=dead  eaded|deadhead=dea
  eaded|deadhead=dead  eaded|deadhead=dead
eaded|deadhead=dead  eaded|deadhead=dead  ea
ded|deadhead=dead  eaded|deadhead=dead  eade
d|deadhead=dead  eaded|deadhead=dead  eaded|
deadhead=dead  eaded|deadhead=dead  eaded|de
adhead=dead  eaded|deadhead=dead  eaded|dea
dhead=dead  eaded|deadhead=dead  eaded|dead
head=dead  eaded|deadhead=dead  eaded|deadh
ead=dead  eaded|deadhead=dead  eaded|deadhea
d=dead  eaded|deadhead=dead  eaded|deadhead
=dead  eaded|deadhead=dead  eaded|deadhead=
dead  eaded|deadhead=dead  eaded|deadhead=de
ad  eaded|deadhead=dead  eaded|deadhead=dea
d  eaded|deadhead=dead  eaded|deadhead=dead
  eaded|deadhead=dead  eaded|deadhead=dead
eaded|deadhead=dead  eaded|deadhead=dead  ea
ded|deadhead=dead  eaded|deadhead=dead  eade
d|deadhead=dead  eaded|deadhead=dead  eaded|
deadhead=dead  eaded|deadhead=dead  eaded|de
adhead=dead  eaded|deadhead=dead  eaded|dea
dhead=dead  eaded|deadhead=dead  eaded|dead
head=dead  eaded|deadhead=dead  eaded|deadh
ead=dead  eaded|deadhead=dead  eaded|deadhea
d=dead  eaded|deadhead=dead  eaded|deadhead
=dead  eaded|deadhead=dead  eaded|deadhead=
dead  eaded|deadhead=dead  eaded|deadhead=de
ad  eaded|deadhead=dead  eaded|deadhead=dea
d  eaded|deadhead=dead  eaded|deadhead=dead
  eaded|deadhead=dead  eaded|deadhead=dead
eaded|deadhead=dead  eaded|deadhead=dead  ea
ded|deadhead=dead  eaded|deadhead=dead  eade
d|deadhead=dead  eaded|deadhead=dead  eaded|
deadhead=dead  eaded|deadhead=dead  eaded|de
adhead=dead  eaded|deadhead=dead  eaded|dea
dhead=dead  eaded|deadhead=dead  eaded|dead
head=dead  eaded|deadhead=dead  eaded|deadh
ead=dead  eaded|deadhead=dead  eaded|deadhea
d=dead  eaded|deadhead=dead  eaded|deadhead
=dead  eaded|deadhead=dead  eaded|deadhead=
dead  eaded|deadhead=dead  eaded|deadhead=de
ad  eaded|deadhead=dead  eaded|deadhead=dead
  eaded|deadhead=dead  eaded|deadhead=dead
eaded|deadhead=dead  eaded|deadhead=dead  ea
ded|deadhead=dead  eaded|deadhead=dead  eade
d|deadhead=dead  eaded|deadhead=dead  eaded|
deadhead=dead  eaded|deadhead=dead  eaded|
```

loss

the memories
the memory
the memo
the

Mike Ferguson is an American permanently resident in the UK. His
most recent poetry publication is the erasure collection *the aran
aphorisms* (Red Ceilings Press, 2024)

Rupert M Loydell

METALLIC INTERLUDES

1. Regression Analysis

A bit of shimmer, shine and novelty sparkle
designed for the modern man.

The robust construction ensures durability,
a perfect fusion of sophistication and street style.

Mother immerses travellers by creating a story
of inner struggles, doubts and failure,

testament to the fact that nought remains.
There are two sides to that argument:

using metasurfaces to create and control *dark* areas
or location, dispersion and shape characterization.

Intelligent idealism: think disintegrate
or a framework for efficient separation.

2. Intelligent Idealism

Designed by creating a metasurface,
shimmer, shine and novelty sparkle
was used to create a story of struggle,
doubts and disintegration. A bit of
location, dispersion and control
allowed for intelligent idealism,
testament to modern man's style
failure and regression analysis.
Shape characterization remains

within the dark areas framework,
robust construction ensures durability,
a calculator fusion of arguments,
perfect to immerse travellers.

3. Disintegration

An intelligent framework:
construction creating control.

CODE FEAR

'I always have a feeling of dread, therefore, when I am on the
point of baring my heart to someone, not because the nakedness
would embarrass me, but rather because I cannot show everything,
simply *cannot*, and must fear being misunderstood because of
this fragmentation.'
  – Heinrich van Kleist, letter to his sister, 1801

Find the rupture caused by life's previous problems,
some of them doubtlessly behind the fear, long-term
vertigo and our own haunting. Fear is about the loss
of time, the transparent membrane of history, change
in response to legitimate threats, a vital riposte to
infectious evolution and the impossibility of feeling
like ourselves. Under the skin, experience often heals
itself and makes our lives more interesting. Fear, on
the other hand, leads to loss of structure and sense.

However, as a motivational force, many neurologists
suggest it allows us to fill up nebulous spaces we find
when building boundaries to avoid possibilities of dis-
placement or separation. Fundamentally, fear translates
association and emotional debris in to emotions which
enable as much guilty pleasure as possible. Erasing fear

means a different path if we get lost between perceptual
borders, since architecture is essentially about space.
Buildings increase the chance of the unknown at home,

fears often associated with a discharge from separating
and putting things in unexpected places. Spaces can be
seen through the margins of psychic perforation but you
should refrain from becoming damaged. The stakes may
be lower today but some individuals still develop extreme
fear from stretched pieces of mind not receptive to ideas.
Meaning and truth may prove to be worse than occasional
bouts of fear before flight but all things scary and spooky
impair people because psychologists cannot define fear.

EXISTENTIAL THREAT NARRATIVE

Resisting the curiosity of playback,
conditions maintained by the genre
allow readers to evidence revolution.

Hardware and mathematics propel us
towards artificial intelligence and
our expedition begins. Beyond risk

opportunities, checkpoint situations,
men, bundles of paper, more controls
than actions. Situations require use,

limit potential, serve to reach truth
or doubt, connect ideas of narrative
to existential threat. Almost everything

hinges on metrics, greater reasoning,
precision microscopes and calculators,
connections between propositions:

the impossible is required. You might be
interested in imagery or literary dynamics,
metaphysical sonnets or the persistence

of vision, may use argument or inference,
speaking and performing in the present;
results do not seem necessary but we must

prepare for romanticism and early flight.
Time instructs youth, reality is essential,
consequence establishes our priorities.

The mind derives from eternal process,
relationships from bodily appearance;
no amount of poetry will turn memory

into lived experience. Internal echoes
may be difficult but the beautiful dance
in question can be immensely pleasurable.

The dullest sensation can become disaster,
the shimmer of trees and inferred meaning
some sort of compensation for our torment.

Justification comes from intent, biases
and limitations which lead to the formation
of all our ideas and consequential actions.

MURDER MYSTERY

A rock band with no rhythm,
this patient's erratic ECG.

An aircraft taking off,
a mountain on fire.

The man down the street
who thinks he is in a sitcom.

A candlelit beach house full
of flowers, birds and tequila.

The woods late at night,
flashlights and dark trees.

Jazz night for old people,
smooth talking in the lift.

True depictions of angels,
those ones with all the eyes.

The annual village dance
and a locked briefcase.

The dramatic revelation
of who the killer is.

FICKLE STATE MACHINE

America. Her boundary. The pressures on all of us
are considerable. Figures fleeing are hard to verify

but war is not popular; modelling dance as a fickle
state machine is reductive, as with any abstraction.

Using graphical models, one can introduce additional
properties but I will save such complexity for another

poem. In the absence of controlled forms, a third
of readers are expected to endure twice more static

than times past, present and future. These have not
turned out to be desirable destinations, just spaces

we move through, narrative sequences we were already
meant to have read, although guys read less generally,

are more in need of films, TV shows and new albums.
The elephant in the room pales in comparison to our

experience of drawing, painting and installation art;
local conditions become literature as humanity is

completely wiped out whilst others seek spare parts
for the hive mind. Dance happens in numerous areas

of the world and you will be safer with finite set moves,
as those tiring practice session people always expect us

to be both positive and fresh. It's surprising but average
temperatures turn out to be invalid within a global

economy if you consider the state we're all in now.
Without exploring, we will assume that boundaries exist,

that there are – obviously – a lot of books and narratives
to drag readers through in any given moment, each time

randomly sequencing the territory. It is simpler than
you think, playing with numbers to again come up with

a complicated sequence of moves, a conceptually infinite
number of nodes in a single chain that travels the same

distance. What you're really witnessing is displacement,
specific actions on a path through a network of context,

a mystic's treatment for white suburban types. Mapping
ought to be a treasure trove for all artificial-intelligence

developers eager to improve human health, yet we tend
to roll our eyes and remain as poorly connected clusters

trying to figure a shortcuts between knowledge and
monetary reward. I wonder where this will end?

Think long, winding sentences, a bunch of independent
systems, stories about things that absolutely matter and

new data all the way. If you tread carefully you will have
a great time. This last line is ambiguous, intentionally so.

Rupert Loydell is the editor of *Stride* magazine, and contributing
editor to *International Times*. He is a widely published poet whose
most recent poetry books are *Damage Limitation* (zimZalla, 2025)
and *The Age of Destruction and Lies* (Shearsman, 2023). He has
edited anthologies for Salt, Shearsman and KFS, written for
academic journals such as *Punk & Post-Punk* (which he is on the
editorial board of), and contributed to books about David Lynch,
Brian Eno and Industrial music.

Elisa A. Garza

Found: Residual Disease Test

Tumor DNA mutation   matched:
     positive risk   for relapse.
Conversely, negative does not   indicate
     absence of   cancer   variation,
     hereditary risk,   new tumors.

Predictive   biomarker   recurrences
assessed by a pathologist,
     margins   and tumor content
     isolated.

Resistance

tumor   mammogram   ultrasound   biopsy
chemo   chemo   chemo   chemo   chemo
immunotherapy   chemo   chemo   chemo
immunotherapy   chemo   chemo
mammogram   ultrasound   chemo
immunotherapy   chemo   chemo   chemo
immunotherapy   chemo   surgery   chemo
radiation   radiation   chemo
radiation   radiation   radiation   radiation
chemo   chemo   mammogram   ultrasound

rash   bruise   biopsy   inflammation   chemo
inflammation   PET scan   chemo   inflammation
chemo   chemo   chemo   chemo   chemo   chemo   chemo
PET scan   surgery   radiation   radiation
ctDNA test   radiation   radiation   radiation

ctDNA test   PET scan   chemo   ctDNA test   chemo ...   ...
.   .   .

Elisa A. Garza is a poet, editor, and writing teacher. Her books include *Regalos* (Lamar University Literary Press), *Between the Light / entre la claridad*, and *Written in the Body* (both from Mouthfeel Press). Her poems have recently appeared in *American Journal of Nursing, Ars Medica, The Acentos Review,* and *Huizache*, who nominated her for the Pushcart Prize.

I wrote these poems during a time when I was experimenting with different poetic forms, both traditional and those of my own devising. I wanted to express the ways cancer and treatments make you feel broken and and out of sorts with reality, even among repetitive tests and treatments that become familiar.

Tobey Hiller

AN ESSAY ON TIME

It was a dark and stormy afternoon. The bedroom held it.

Outside, the slough was goosebelly silver and the

meadow reflected greenish light; inside the air hung

blurred, fogged with words. The color of this had no

feathers.

It was a dark and stormy moment. Would it pass?

Moments are eager to go, though some return. The

drumbeat of this one rippled into the room's time, which,

like the sea, had tides.

The question is going to be where to find the beginning.

The middle's easy—we're always in it. Until the end, of

course—when the middle coagulates into a story already

told, in versions. It's the beginning that disappears over

an event horizon that might be, when you take a good

look, dark and stormy. Or, blink again, on the other hand

dazzling, in fact auroral. Dawn's a daily story, married,

as eye to eyelid, to dusk. There are different views, it's

clear, and they're not limited to these two moments of

growing or fading light—you can't escape variety in the

landscape. It's time that unrolls the conundrums.

In this dark and stormy moment, she thought mainly of

escape, or a quiet that resembled torpor, the scent, for

instance, of tropical ginger. His voice like a helmet she

wished to remove. He thought mainly of his fury, his

chest and throat, what she was costing him. He regarded

himself as a man who kept his eye on the ball, not as a

man beside himself. She thought of herself sometimes,

and possibly in this moment, as a bird or cat, two

creatures, you will note, whose cohabitation works only

when there's plenty of room. No doubt they both had

their reasons, or at least

some map for the pathways they'd followed into this

moment; still, reason is rarely a feature of conflict. She

felt his pathway narrow and rocky, with walls that cut off

a wider view. He was not interested in any goddamn

pathway metaphor.

It may be pertinent here to mention the trembling gap

between stories and lies. And the fact that time is factless

and unwinged. Stories ride it; lies like it too. That no

philosophy comforts, unlike trees. Are these dark and

stormy thoughts? Not the tree part. I am doing the best I

can, with the words time has given me. They gather in

tribes, like moments. As for stories, some lope along, or

tick and then explode. Some know what a galliard is, or a

joke, and I prefer these, to tell the truth. They are all

around us, revealed on time's uncalendared skin. Lies,

too, hatch constantly, though you might be able to tell

them by the

fact that their eggs stink. Of course, that's true of some facts, too.

So now, you see, as always happens in the grip of time, we are confused.

In this dark and stormy moment, she thought mainly of another life, with a scent like tropical ginger. What he thought had no scent and was all airborne, reverberating in its own life. They both thought mainly of themselves as misunderstood. The easy cohabitation of the past and the future clashed in this moment's velocity, despite earlier clues to the contrary. To both of them, this made the room seem smaller than the emotional space required. She watched some shadow disappear around a corner that did not exist. The door he was about to slam stepped forward. This was no surprise to either of them. No doubt they both had their reasons, or at least some map for the pathways they'd followed into this moment; still, reason is so rarely a feature of connection, which, like

time, is a conundrum, and has tides. She felt his current

reasons narrow and rocky, with walls that cut off a wider

view. He was not interested in her reasons at all.

But I am repeating myself, more or less.

Looking at a room blurred with time, you may glimpse

the specks and glitters of multiple moments—these

include many stories, any lies, the prickly touch of some

dark unknown, and the breast of truth, feathered yes and

breathing, such a fragile bird, so soon flown. Time, then,

as a skin, a nest, a figment. Perhaps it seems a

whirlwind, or a musical chord, or simply a cave where

you need a flashlight to see the markings.

Even in the matter of love, which also has its tides, its

imperatives, its desertions of the expected physics, you

need a flashlight to see the markings. So often illegible,

despite all the sonnets. She had meant to tell him that,

but did not find the words, just as he had meant to tell

her where to find the ball, which had rolled under some

table somewhere in the course of dinner and lost its way.

Time's hand appears everywhere. Though of course time

has no hand. Or skin, etc. It is not even an equation at the

speed of light. Always the inescapable language of our

own bodies. Time has no body, though our bodies tick

with time's blood pulse. It does not run, or stop or wait,

or hold, or die or breathe or wonder. Or love. But we are

lost in it as completely as if it were a body much larger

than ours, say a

sea. A sea offering what seems an endless immersion
that ends, finally, on the rocks or sand.

When he turned toward the door, the hand of an invisible

heft, perhaps feathered but stubborn, brushed him back.

Or perhaps it was the disappeared ball, landing hard

between the blades of his mind's shoulders. So he made

instead a bargain with his mouth, to let no words pass,

for how many hours he did not count or imagine. He

would consider the word "pathway," which had come to

him as an emanation of dusk's air. She, meanwhile,

watched the goosebelly silver of the slough turn blue,

and at the bluest moment, all pathways seemed ready to

lead to the curiosities and certitudes of Rome, beckoning.

Though no destination was needed, and no map, only this

blue. She felt him standing still, as the door, through

which evening blew in, turned into time, which has no

direction.

You will note that words run away like love or time,

even though you can read them over and think they've

helped you snag a stitch of stillness. What enters you is

feathered. Another of time's conundrums. Being made of

time, I cannot help trying to say it. Just like you, I can

only assume. While I count the fingers on the past's left

hand, the right hand holds up the goodbye of things.

A color of invisible feathers in which we fly.

time equals but is nothing the same as

rock

river   orbit

constellated space

a thrown baseball   the doeppler effect

and

whale fall

whose bodies falling full fathom five

to a deep we cannot survive

harbor whole civilizations   teeming

cities   forests

of small creatures, blooms and biologies

we cannot imagine

time is nothing that comes after *is*
it is something that comes after *be*..

THE BATH

Many nights she took a bath, late. By that time things were over
She closed the door to the bathroom, drew the bath, and lay back in
the warm waters, subsiding into another medium than the day's
piled-up hours. As though—she did not *think* this, just knew it in
the water's lip and smooth—to be engulfed in a cloud of her own
unknowing. Unknowing, that is, about anywhere but right here,
unknowing about noon or morning insistence, other rooms and
their corners, lists, hullabaloo minor or major.

Warm float, that's all she wanted. She dreamed the door to the
bathroom a moat, the cloud of thoughtlessness a bulwark of handy
air. Handfuls of calm. First the rushing sound of the tub filling.
Then quiet, a few drips from the faucet, which in these moments
had a plucked but soft sound of mermaid melody, a feel of melt on
a watery edge. Occasional lapping sounds when she moved. Tides.
Her mind would empty as she lay in the water, eyes closed. She
always put a washcloth soaked in the hot bath water over her
exposed chest to keep it warm. Her mother, who had not taught her
much that was useful, had taught her this trick, and when she laid

on the washcloth, her mother invariably came to mind. Also when she saw certain blues. Her mother had loved a particular blue whose name she could no longer remember—it may have begun with an a or a p—or maybe some other runaway letter—but was neither azure nor periwinkle and had now disappeared into a nameless ocean of muted blues—like so much about her mother, who had been so, yes, blue. For years she herself had never worn blue. Silly. The water in the tub, a faint greenish color, was far from the triumph of lapis seas, of course. Different waters everywhere, a reminder.

When the washcloth cooled, she warmed it again in the water and laid it down, a comfort to her heart, once more. Her hands floated. The cloth weighed down her breasts with warmth. She lay unmoving for long minutes, in the embrace of what seemed a heavier and kinder air. A kind of sensate music. Sometimes she dozed. It was always hard to make the decision to get out, but. But next was always there, so eventually she'd wash herself and climb out, towel off, apply cream, brush her teeth, all that stuff. It was the bath that counted. The bath that offered a little door, like a creek carrying your thoughts around a bend, to something she didn't even have to name.

Maybe three nights out of seven she managed this. Not every night worked—hard, often, to fit it in, what with life's imperatives outside the bathroom. She did not think of the bath and its soothing waters, though, as an escape, more as a right, a bonded pleasure, a sinking into water's cerulean music, a respite too often shortchanged by schedules and stridencies—of hurry and plan, the demands, both explicit and implicate, others made on her, anticipation's push or strive, the news, her own hopes unfurled like flags, the hours that tolled and beeped, devices that reminded. It all spoke and trilled and buzzed and clicked. Or shouted. Far too much noise and muscle in every air. Too hard to hear the other music.

The frequency changed. It became four nights out of seven, and then, over time, five. The baths became longer; she had begun to lock the door, though,f or reasons having to do with the time of night, knocking was rare.

It was how to come and go, daily, that snagged every moment. How to stay or say. Or not. But in the waters of the bath what wandered in and out of mind's air, or flew away to roost somewhere, in its own froth, splash or ripple, grew easy. She craved this more and more, like food or sleep or sky's free clouds. No sharp tangles occurred in the bath. An evening ocean, and she lay in a little ship on waters that did not insist on travel. Yet.

It was the day she filled the tub so full it began to splash over on to the floor she had just that morning mopped that she realized the ship had set full sail.

At last, she thought. A simple motion, neap tide and all in balance. She rose out of the tub, dried herself, applied the usual cream, dressed, and walked out of the bathroom and straight out the front door, leaving the aqua mermaid sheen of her wet footprints on the bathroom floor, where they dried before anyone saw them.

Peripheral Vision

A black shadow—ghost crow? flies up,
the moon's eyelash trembles, per
ception rights itself, shakes a blurred shoulder.
I look ahead into white tumble of plum bloom.

Sideways and under, vision tells stories flanged
with light's dark blink, obscure wonders or warnings,
molecules not shaped for names. Glimpse melts. In
the window's corner, summer's avatar flings glitter.

Sidewise, from off stage, the future present enters,
shedding all grammar. Gaze glides wide. Squint's
genius for shape gathers clarity's dream. Edge's
edgy jitter gathers voice for some distant harmony

or noise of next, like that time the stars still
burned, swirled their epic unwords of time
far far from our blink of now, out
at the brim of notice, where knowledge thins.

Discursions

Neptune and Uranus are blue, wrapped in scarves of methane.

In the airport, a woman walks a tortoise-shell cat on a leash.

On the California coast, a wooden house slides down a hill.

Some distant planets have storms of glass rain.

On a sidewalk in NYC, a woman 68 years old freezes to death.

Unsolved math problem: why do certain chords make us want to weep?

The cat at the airport says something in cat.

On our sun, only a small star, a great wind of fire blows without cease.

We don't know what we don't know.

Time travel happens every night—leaving our bodies requires only dream's alchemy.

In math's universe, you can't make two by cutting one in half.

If you can explain war to children, you are dead.

The art of art contains no irreplaceable elements except the salt of tears, imagination's fat,

and unfolding's muscular insistence, yet again.

When the lights go off and the music stops, where's the sky?

When the end comes, dancing is optional but possible.

The cat in the airport understands the leash's length but does not approve.

No one needs to tell you to breathe—

it's as easy as floating between one shore and another,

if you see my meaning's float.

At midnight we may mistake dark for the light of reason.

Who's to say what cows are thinking, or how orchestral the green

of forest oxygen—though milk, lungs and clouds are clues.

The sound of traffic can resemble a beehive's hum,
but it doesn't rise to clouds as honey.
Smiling for the camera is something no child is born to do.
How many of us will make the planet lose its balance?
It does not take a human being to hear a forest's hum and speech.
Perhaps cats know this. Certainly birds.

Could we be birds? Light? Prairie? Granite? Concrete?
Wind?

A Little Collation

Ducks' tongues: perhaps it never occurred to you such a dish
　　　　might appear before you on the table.

When it does, and you try it, does that make your dreams
　　　　inexplicably sharp and strange,
　　　　with a little scratched striation down the
　　　　middle of each thought that signifies
　　　　how carnage and delicacy
　　　　mix themselves in human mouths?

In the wet mud of the half-roofed shed, innumerable pocks
　　　　of rain where the horses have stood.
　　　　On the phone I say, meddlesomely,
　　　　horses need dry shelter. I mention
　　　　hoof rot. *They're fine, thanks.* A
　　　　pock of silence, then a click
　　　　on the other end of the line.

In the dark, using a flashlight, we pull
    hay for the mud-caked, whinnying horses
    and I know there is little shelter
    in words.

In the cabin, the evening floats, round bubble of dry and glowing
    warmth inside this place
    where much is ordered
    as it should be
    and as we desire.

This small domain is neither illusion nor
    truth. Its being cannot threaten
    the world's sorrow but still it lies
    in the mouth of such a world, sweet
    as green grass at noon,
    striated, scratching.

In Praise of Form

entranced by the form and build of things,
the spirals, loops, planks and sediments, the rings

I feel my heart's insistent hand beat slow
as ticked or wide or green as fluttered leaf the moments go

or is that just the glow, time's always flow, the wild
of onward's beckon, eternal scribe

of what is ever changing, the here's
now, erosion's plow, calendar of blood, a sheer

shoreline marking pluck and pulse so fleet
no mind can hold or frame it, no mountain matter meet

any replicate of this instant's brush, or folded wing of then
despite memory, dream, meditation, hope or Zen

memory will tell you something scribbled in the dark
of possible light, shadowed with the past's odd arc

of wounds, wilds, storms, lights of noon and brights of fall,
so touch form's dazzling carapace, touch as you can, the all

right now, it's here, though when I use the indeterminate *it*
no god but time will tell its story, which is (I say) *dit dit dit*

TOBEY HILLER writes poetry, flash, and fiction—her
publications include four books of poetry, a novel, individual
stories and flash, and a collection of surreal/fabulist stories,
FLIGHT ADVICE: A FABULARY (Unlikely Books, 2022), the
latter a finalist for an Omnidawn Fabulist Fiction award. Her
poems and stories have appeared widely in journals, such as
*Abraxas, Ambush Review, AbleMuse, Askew, Calaban, Canary,
Catamaran Literary Reader, CRAFT, En*trance* (the debut issue),
The Fabulist: Words & Art, Shotglass Journal (MusePie Press),
*Here Comes Everyone (HCE), 5 Fingers Review, Mediterranean
Poetry, The MacGuffin, Milkweed Chronicle, North Coast Literary
Review, The Orchards Journal, Persimmon, Poetry Flash, The
Racket, Sisyphus, Sin Fronteras/Writers without Borders, Spillway,
Unlikely Stories Mark V* and others, as well as in eight
anthologies:, including *FIRE AND*

RAIN: ECOPOETRY OF CALIFORNIA (Scarlet Tanager Press), a number of West Coast anthologies, *ARRIVING AT A SHORELINE* (great weather for MEDIA, 2022, New York) and *BEACON RADIANT* (great weather for MEDIA, 2024, New York). Recently, four of her flash & short prose pieces appeared in Ravenna Press's *TRIPLE SERIES (no. 21, 2023)*. Her most recent book of poems, *CROW MIND*, is reviewed in "The Los Angeles Review" at http://losangelesreview.org/review-crow-mind-tobey-hiller/

Both her poems and short stories have won magazine and contest awards.

Her current poetry ms. *BEFORE ANYTHING IS DUST* was named one of three finalists in *CATAMARAN LITERARY READER'S 2024 Poetry Book Contest*.

An Artistic Statement*

My focus in my work is on the various ecologies of relationship we inhabit in all our worlds: urban, rural, intimate, emotional/intellectual.. And in the relation of self to self, with the self's changing stories amid the shifting architectures of time. Our lives change us. We're somewhat like language itself, which is pressed into constant new shapes by its surroundings. The networks in which we live are not really distinct. The contact between these different spheres of experience, sometimes grinding, sometimes smooth—i.e. both violent and melting—is inevitably organic and seismic. This complicated skein is not really different from the body's neurological wholeness. We don't just live in a changing landscape; we are one. A territory where familial, political, historical and spiritual states create the gravity that molds our lives. And between the inwardness and outwardness of our lives lies a bridge we(I) yearn to navigate with art. Writing, music, the visual arts, the creative act—want to touch that space, map it, reveal it, if only for a moment, and never with complete success.

Formally, I'm drawn to a variety of forms, often hybrid, where different effects are possible and language stretches constantly, where signifiers and genres blend and clash and melt. Transformations. The ordinary's grand strangeness. As in the world's geologies, or the way a riverine environment exists as a blend of water and land life, liquid and solid and all that lives between. Very fertile areas: intersections and edges, where one comes upon new discoveries.

Discovery and connection are the goals of my art. I have a longtime interest in myth, legend, fable, where awe still resides. As a species, what distinguishes us is not language—there's a lot of that out there in the lives of other animals—but story-making. The urge to make a mark on time's wall, whether palm or word.

* N.B. I only know these things because I've been writing now for a long time, and the writing itself, and the other creative things I do, have taught me why I do them. I did not start working from these ideas. They captured me.

J. D. Nelson

in the shelter headphones gentlemen headphones

...

sun chips sink ships

...

grapes
bananas
spider rings

...

brain zaps

zzt-zzt-zzt

zzt-zzt-zzt

zzt-zzt-zzt

...

clouds moon there you go

...

fedex guy blasts cantina theme holy saturday

...

peroxide on a scratch açai juice

...

out / in
this

...

amok at wa(lma)rt wet-eyed ringo

...

dreamland narrowly no frog bacon

...

blue butter relaxer flicker tonight's metro

...

but spidey lawn chair we papered

...

bus stn bat blue & gold dinner

...

buffalo'd better lungs of hell outloved

...

heretofore slow-roasted qr codes zetro etc.

...

a
or a
ouray

...

+ vole
me or me

...

alone at it genes [in an en] velope

...

rold gold opinionated marin alsop

...

spock's minty feetfloss expeller-pressed mtns

...

no kind of sidewalk ringtone wormy

...

purple irides sway panic attack!

...

there's the ghost of 30th street no sheet

...

brushbuilt alum salad calm-to-be crow

...

J. D. Nelson (b. 1971) is the author of twelve collections of poetry, including *Cinderella City* (The Red Ceilings Press, 2012). Visit MadVerse.com for more information and links to his published work. Nelson lives in Boulder, Colorado, USA.

About the Poems

In addition to Dada and Surrealism, my work is greatly influenced by Japanese short-form poetry, especially haiku.

Nikhil Harle

i moon in vacuum

(

ii awakenings

i broke the membrane–

  <the boundary, like a black hole's event horizon>

–of poetry at last.

it was not through sound–

  <not the drumbeats and plops
  of plosive consonants
  nor the soothing caresses
  of sibilant fricatives>

–no, not through rhyme and rhythm's marriage.

it was not through vision–

  <not closing my eyes and feeling the breeze
  kiss whitman's blades of grass;
  nor gazing o'er the undergrowth
  on frost's untaken path>

–no, not through imagination's cinema.

it was through a beautiful theory–

  < (
  this is the space of poetry>

–called ~quantum electrodynamics~.

Q.E.D.

) >

iii the beautiful theory of ~quantum electrodynamics~

the world is all just a puzzle, you know–
seas of electrons wandering through all the possible paths.
not unlike how at night we walk through landscape-flickers
the self-constructing architecture of dream.

these poems are all just puzzles too, you know–
words like small wood ink-symbol blocks
to be arranged in nice, straight rows and columns
and translated to electrical signals in your brain.

would you like to…
…connect the circuit?
(with me?)

[if not, cue end of poem]

in you : observe the order put pieces what when happens ?

what ? |*thein:orderpieces*| when you |*observehappensput*|

pieces in you |*observetheorderput*| what happens? when

what happens |*whenthepiecesputyouinorder*|? observe:

observe: what happens when you put the pieces in order?

iv vacuum in moon

```
        _____
   /              \

 |        (0)        |

   \              /
        _____
```

v lullaby

it makes me happy, you know,
knowing that you trust me like this.

(

may i say something to you?

          [if not, cue end of poem]

    you-
       -are*
         *enough–
         *more than enough–
       -don't have to prove anything to&
                    &me
                    &or anyone.
    just:
       :be here
       :right now
       :on the page
       :in the space we make
    when{
     i arrange words on *paper*
        lamplight hits *paper*
              paper
       emits

light====
=guided by your cornea
=filtered by your lens
=electrified by your retina
=chauffeured up your optic nerve

and somewhere, tangled–
across the circuitry of your brain
there is
poetry

`breath in` ——— `audible sigh`

imagine.
.a soft blanket around you, right now
.warm and cozy
.pulling you in

how does *that* feel?
?warm?
?safe?
?like nothing can touch you whilst
in the page?
?this tangled web of electricity
in your brain
?will keep the world away for a while
?just for`
`you
`a while

you#
#deserve that.
#deserve%
%every
%little

%bit
%of care
%and more
#have no idea, reader–
                    –how much i adore you.

Nikhil Kiran Harle is a PhD student in physics at JILA and an opera singer. He was formerly Artistic Director of the Opera Theater of Yale College. Recent poetry appears in *The Winged Moon.*

Concept note
As a physicist, I am very interested in the concept of emergent phenomena, for example, by which complex behavior emerges from simple rules and building blocks. The enjoyment of poetry to me is such a phenomena, and I experiment with symbols, spacing and syntax to explore the process by which meaning is produced by lines and dots on paper.

Mark Cunningham

from/to **FLYCATCHER**

speciflick
thinge

glimmere?
glimear?
beleaf?

multirude

memeory

synnap

pleathora
voidce

vocull
volube
throwat

hesistate

infearior

hazairdust

emurge

appropriot

coherunt
vertebrat

(gl)itch

knoise

saime

detrituse

ru*ssh*

enviroff

Mark Cunningham's most recent book is gu(e)st (g)host from
Sandy Press. A new collection, Fleshwater, will be available from
Lulu soon.

Jonathan Cant

Death Notice

Today as I wandered,
I wondered if I were
dead. People, buried
deep in their phones,
jostled me as if I
wasn't seen. So, I
waited around and
leaned against a post;
expecting someone to
walk right through me
(like Patrick Swayze
in *Ghost*) when I had
a kind of awakening.
These days, *death* is
just not being noticed.

Two Lines

'MADE
IN U.S.A.'
says the
single
edge
blade.
'Surgical
steel.
Industrial
grade.'
Strength and
sharpness,
will bring
me the same.
Surely
a razor
erases
a name!
States
that it's:
'Handy for
removing
all labels'.
You like
the way that
it scrapes
across
tables.

You
chop,
you
chisel,
you coax
and corral.
So fine
the crystals,
so high
the morale.
Already racing,
your heart's
a balloon.
Time to
cue up
a familiar
tune.
Like a
powdery
PAUSE
button,
two lines
lay...
a brief
hesitation
...then
you push
PLAY.

Tricube 27 (a 3x3x3)

There's a "club"
for dead rock
musicians:

Hendrix, Jim
Morrison,
and Janis.

Their years now
spent—like these
syllables.

Aubade for an Arm

Parting is such sweet sorrow—Shakespeare

You wake in fright to a terrible sight,
When you realise how you've spent the night.

Your arm is stuck under a stranger's head—
Not wanting to wake them, you're filled with dread.

You weigh up your options. What *can* you do?
You bite on your arm and begin to chew!

The Tower

I

X

Eiffel

X

X

Eye full

X X

X X

I fall! I fall!

X X X

X X X

X X X

X X X X

X X X X X X

X X X X X X X

Awful.   Awful.   Awful.

Jonathan Cant is a writer, poet, and musician. His work has: been shortlisted in the 2025 Gwen Harwood Poetry Prize; won the 2023 Banjo Paterson Writing Awards for Contemporary Poetry; and was longlisted for the 2023 Fish Poetry Prize. His poems have appeared in *Cordite, Island, Verandah, Otoliths, and Live Encounters.*

Artist Statement:

Death Notice places the concrete/shape poem in the obituaries section at the back of the newspaper; but, then (as the poem explores), not all "deaths" kill you completely.

Two Lines is another concrete/shape poem that takes on the appearance of its subject.

Tricube 27 (a 3x3x3) employs a relatively new form of poetry invented by Philip Larrea in 2001. The "tricube" consists of three stanzas of three lines of three syllables each; where each stanza contains a complete thought or idea and is resolved in the last.

Aubade for an Arm is an absurdist parody of the traditional "aubade" form. Just as the "nocturne" explores nighttime themes like romance, love, and lust, the "aubade" concerns itself with morning matters such as reluctantly bidding a lover farewell or, in this case, going out of one's way to not do so.

The Tower is a concrete/shape poem that also stretches the phonetic possibilities of a single word to convey the story.

Mark Blaeuer

Jeopardy at Dawn

Sunlight through
an east window, orienting.
On terminal, an eager
shill:

"Death Whistle Blowout Sale!"
The very thing craved,
a skull-shape ocarina from Tenochtitlán.
Toss to host.

"The answer is . . .
He woke in a good mood, which lasted until
an Aztec priest slit open his abdomen,
plunged one arm blindly in,

reaching past diaphragm
for the organ of fit sacrifice—
and triumphantly yanked out
a red rhythm."

Mark Blaeuer's poems have appeared in 100+ journals, including *Bone Orchard, The Charleston Anvil, Ink Sweat & Tears, Nude Bruce Review, Otoliths, Stink Eye Magazine,* and *Uut.* His collections are *Fragments of a Nocturne* (Kelsay, 2014) and *Surfacing Below* (SurVision, 2025). He lives near Hot Springs, Arkansas.

Eileen Tabios

The American Center in Moscow Meets Eileen R. Tabios

Meet a Poet	*Познакомьтесь с поэтом*
EILEEN R. TABIOS	АЙЛИН ТАБИОС
Sixteen poems	Шестнадцать стихотворений
Translated by Anna Krushelnitskaya	Перевод с английского Анны Крушельницкой
Presented by The American Center, Moscow November 21, 2022	Представляет Американский центр, Москва 21 ноября 2022 года

Translator :

Anna Krushelnitskaya   is a translator, writer, and language teacher. Her articles on foreign language pedagogy appeared in *Modern English Teacher* and *ESL Magazine*, as well as in scholarly journals in Russia. Anna's translations were featured in *Poems from the Front* (Moscow, 2020); *Disbelief: 100 Russian Anti-War Poems* (Smokestack, 2022), and a variety of print and online magazines and literary journals, such as *Russian Life*, *Plume*, *South Florida Poetry Journal*, *5th Wave*, *Circumference* and more. Her most recent book-length publications include *Firefly in a Box: An Anthology of Soviet Kid Lit* (co-edited with Dmitri Manin; UPM, 2025), *Dislocation: An Anthology of Poetic Response to Russia's War in Ukraine* (co-edited with Julia Nemirovskaya; Slavica, 2024) and *Babi Yar and Other Poems by Ilya Ehrenburg* (with introduction by Joshua Rubenstein; Smokestack, 2024). Anna's favorite past solo project is the 2019 *Cold War Casual*, a bilingual collection of oral testimony reflecting on the effects of the events and the government propaganda of the Cold War era on daily lives and mindsets of regular citizens of countries on both sides of the Iron Curtain.

If Love, Then Love

—excavated from "The Professor and the Madman," a movie history of the Oxford English Dictionary

I.
All I need are books.

Every word in action becomes beautiful in the light of its own meaning.

When I read, no one is after me. When I read, I am the one who is chasing, chasing after God.

What I know of love: the sickness often becomes the cure.

The brain is wider than the sky...

II.
"I can, because of you."

III.
Madness gave us words.

Sometimes when we push away, that's when we need to be resisted.

IV.
I wanted to document the history of each and everything, to offer the world a book that gives a meaning of everything in God's creation.

Если любовь, то любовь

—откопано в «Профессоре и безумце», киноистории Оксфордского словаря английского языка

I.
Мне нужны только книги.

Каждое слово в действии становится прекрасным в свете своего значения.

Когда я читаю, никто не гонится за мной. Когда я читаю, это я гонюсь, гонюсь за Господом.

Вот что я знаю о любви: болезнь часто становится лекарством.

Мозг шире неба...

II.
«Я могу, из-за тебя».

III.
Безумие дало нам слова.

Иногда мы отталкиваем от себя; как раз тогда нам нельзя этого позволять.

IV.
Я хотела запечатлеть историю всего и каждого, представить миру книгу, истолковывающую значение всего в творении Божьем.

V.
The book—it's not yours to quit.

I know the answer to the widow's question.

Maganda Begins

> "Maganda" is not just a Tagalog word that means "beautiful". "Maganda" is also the name of the first woman in a Filipino creation myth.

My love. If
words can
reach

whatever world you
suffer in—
Listen:

I have things
to tell
you.
At this muffled
end to
another

year, I prowl
somber streets
holding

you—in my
head, this
violence!—

V.
Эта книга – не тебе ее бросать.

Я знаю ответ на вопрос вдовы.

Начало Маганды

> «Маганда» — не просто слово, означающее «красивая» в тагальском языке. Маганда – имя первой женщины в филиппинской легенде о сотворении мира.

Мой любимый. Если
слова смогут
добраться

до той вселенной,
где страдаешь –
Слушай:

Мне есть что
сказать сейчас
тебе.
В этом глухом
конце еще
одного

года, я обшариваю
хмурые улицы,
держа

тебя – в своей
голове, такая
жестокость! –

a violent gaze.	такой жестокий взгляд.
You. With	Ты. После
dusk	заката
arrives rain drifting	приходит дождь, идущий
aslant like	косо, как
premature	незрелое
memory. Am I	воспоминание. Я ли
the one	та самая,
who	кто
suddenly cleared these	внезапно очистил эти
streets? *My*	улицы? *Мой*
Love,	*Любимый,*
all our hours	каждый наш час
are curfew	есть комендантский
hours—	час –
what I offer	я могу предложить
is this	только эту
dying	умирающую
fish into whose	рыбу, в чьи
gullet I	жабры я
have	уже
thrust my thumb.	засунула большой палец.
Why did	Почему же
you	ты
lose all Alleluias?	утратил все аллилуйи?
My love—	*Мой любимый* –
Listen:	Слушай:

Weather Du Jour

blueness
of sky—
I am breathing

After Chazal

Sunflowers
release gold—
dust of illusion

[Note: *Antoine Chazal (8
November 1793 in Paris – 12
August 1854 in Paris) was a
French painter of flowers and of
portraits and engraver]*

Athena

What's deemed necessary
changes. Hear
me

listening in another
decade, editing
last

and first lines.
A different
Singer

croons from behind
an impassive
speaker.

I listen, cross
out more
lines.

Погода Du Jour

синева
этого неба –
и я дышу

По мотивам Шазаля

Подсолнухи
испускают золото –
пыль от иллюзий

[Примечание: Антуан Шазаль (8
ноября 1793, Париж – 12
августа 1854, Париж) был
французским гравером и
художником, рисовавшим цветы
и портреты]

Афина

То, что необходимо,
меняется. Слышишь,
я

слушаю в другом
десятилетии, правлю
последние

и первые строки.
Уже другой
Певец

поет из-за спины
совсем бесстрастного
динамика.

Я слушаю, вычеркиваю
еще больше
строк.

The poem cannot
be pure.
Sound

never travels unimpeded
by anonymous
butterflies.

Writing it down
merely freezes
flight—

Translation: an inevitable
fall. Take
control
by shooting it
as if
pigeons

were clay: This
one is.
But

it provided pleasure
once, was
"necessary."

Once, it flew
with non-imaginary
wings.

O, clay pigeon.
Translation: the
error

is my ear's.
The sky
ruptured

Стихотворение не может
быть безупречным.
Звук

всегда проходит заграждения
из анонимных
бабочек.

Запись его словами
просто замораживает
полет –

Перевод: это неизбежное
падение. Держи
контроль,
стреляй так, как
будто это
голуби

из глины: Этот
правда такой.
Но

он доставлял удовольствие
когда-то, был
«необходим».

Когда-то он летал
на невыдуманных
крыльях.

О, голубь глиняный.
Перевод: эта
ошибка

сделана моим ухом.
С небес
прорвалось

suddenly—I saw
but did
not

hear the precursor
fall of
leaves.

***

Edit it down.
Edit it
down.

Silence is Queen,
not lady
-in-waiting.

Edit it down.
Edit it.
Edit

it down. Edit
it. Edit.
Edit.

внезапно – я увидела,
но я
не

шороха падающей
листвы.

***

Сокращай и вычеркивай.
Сокращай и
вычеркивай.

Молчание – это королева,
не придворная
дама.

Вычеркивай и сокращай.
Вычеркивай и
сокращай.

И вычеркивай. И
сокращай. И
Вычеркивай.

From "147 Million Orphans," MMXIII

*television
screening insightful
prescient melancholy evasive*

If you were a sleeping bird in Madagascar, a certain species of moth might drink your tears through a fearsome proboscis shaped like a harpoon. They'd insert their tools beneath your eyelids. They would drink *avidly.* You were a rapt presence as you met this species through the grainy television screen used to babysit hundreds of orphans. After the television darkened, no genius would be required to explain your prescient conclusion: you will attempt to evade too much in this life, you will fail, *there is no other life.* Your insights will always arise from the sheen of rain-drenched pavements. For example, that one can weep without the aid of nightmares—that one can weep in the safest haven, or even the small heavens that still and do manage to pock-mark our mortal planet.

Из «147 миллионов сирот», MMXIII

*телевидение
просмотр проницательно
пророческий меланхолия
уклончиво*

Если бы вы были спящей птицей в Мадагаскаре, мотыли определенного вида могли бы пить ваши слезы своими пугающими гарпунообразными хоботками. Они втыкали бы свои инструменты вам под веки. Они пили бы *жадно.* Вы завороженно присутствовали при встрече с этим видом через зернистое изображение на телеэкране, который работал нянькой сотен сирот. Когда телевизор погас, даже не гений смог бы объяснить ваше пророческое заключение: вы попытаетесь уклониться от слишком многого в жизни, вам не удастся, *другой жизни не будет.* Ваши прозрения будут всегда прорастать из блеска залитых дождем мостовых. Например, что можно плакать без помощи ночных кошмаров – можно плакать в надежнейшем убежище, и даже в маленьком раю, которыми всё еще и всё же испещрена наша смертная планета.

From "147 Million Orphans," MMXVII

endowed
faith catapulted
perplexed coddle pamper

The one who has never been coddled was informed she would be adopted and she cried out in response, *THANK YOU SO MUCH!* We mothers hate hearing this story—no child should learn to be grateful for an effect of loss. Yes, we can understand why she is grateful. But no child should learn to be grateful for an effect of loss. This is an example of how perplexity can be the most appropriate reaction. Her new
for a camera—perhaps what unfolds will become real for her only when affirmed by photographs, objects she can touch and recover. She's learned at too young an age that memory is fragile and lapses too often to desire. Because my faith has not yet betrayed, I see her easily in my mind's eye as frolicking on what could be a Hollywood movie set of beige sand, blue water, green mountain, a grove of palm trees, looking back frequently at her new Mom to grin, carefully tip-toeing around the delicate sea creatures laid on sand by an ocean calmed from witnessing her eager joy, looking back frequently at me. I will be calling out, *Be careful. Have fun. Yes, it's all lovely.*

Из «147 миллионов сирот», MMXVII

одарен
вера катапультирована
озадачен кутать баловать

Та, которую никогда не баловали, была извещена, что ее удочерят, и расплакалась в ответ: ОГРОМНОЕ СПАСИБО! Мы, матери, терпеть не можем таких историй – дети не должны учиться благодарности за последствия потерь. Да, мы понимаем, почему она благодарна. Но дети не должны учиться благодарности за последствия потерь. Это пример того, как растерянность может быть самой подходящей реакцией. Ее новая мать сказала ей, что семья возьмет ее с собой в отпуск. Она попросила фотоаппарат – возможно, все, что произойдет, станет реальным для нее только тогда, когда утвердится в фотографии, предмете, который она сможет потрогать и восстановить. В чересчур раннем возрасте она узнала, что память хрупка и провалы в ней случаются чаще, чем хочется. Поскольку вера еще не предала меня, я с легкостью вижу своим внутренним взором, как она резвится на фоне чего-то наподобие голливудской декорации к фильму, с бежевым песком, синей водой, зеленой

горой, пальмовой рощей,
постоянно оборачиваясь, чтобы
улыбнуться своей новой маме,
осторожно обходя на цыпочках
хрупкие морские создания,
разложенные на песке океаном,
утихомиренным тем, как она
готовно радуется, постоянно
оборачиваясь ко мне. Я крикну
ей, *Осторожно. Иди поиграй.
Да, просто прелестно.*

From "147 Million Orphans," MMXLIII

clad
rubbing corroborate
cursory dehydrate derive

Press paper against a street
etching. Rub graphite against the
paper. Your fingers feel the grit
but ... What does the rubbing
corroborate? Is not the souvenir
of pain mere derivative of the
authentic? Entonces, let us not
be cursory. The parched will tell
you, *Avoid cladding us with
words.*

Из «147 миллионов сирот», MMXLIII

облачён
трение подтвердить
бегло обезводить извлечь

Прижмите бумагу к уличному
барельефу. Потрите графитом
по бумаге. Ваши пальцы ощутят
грубую поверхность, но... Что
подтверждает трение? Разве
этот сувенир боли не простое
производное от настоящего?
Entonces, давайте не бегло.
Иссушенные скажут вам,
*Избегайте облекать нас в
слова.*

The Singer

When they heard
him, they
heard

the whips over
his ancestors
as

they were forced
out from
India.

They heard a
man thrown
into

jail for stealing
a small
bunch

of grapes, then
the ugly
grunts

of his starving
wife and
children.

When they heard
him, they
heard

a shivering woman
with no
defense

Певец

Когда они услышали
его, они
услышали

как свистели плети
над его
предками

которых гнали прочь
из родной
Индии.

Они услышали, как
человека бросают
в

тюрьму за кражу
одной малой
грозди

винограда, а потом
как некрасиво
кряхтят

от голода его
жена и
дети.

Когда они услышали
его, они
услышали

как дрожит женщина
не имея
защиты

as the soldiers came to do	от тех солдат которые пришли сделать
what they did with her and	то что сделали с ней и
her still too-young daughters." They heard	с её маленькими дочерьми. Они услышали
the stars fall into bleak silence.	как падают звезды в мрачную тишину.
When they heard him, they heard	Когда они услышали его, они услышали
his *cante* come from him like	как его *cante* выходит из него
a rusty nail being pulled from	как ржавый гвоздь который тянут из
an old board. *La voz* *afilla—*	старой деревянной доски. *La voz* *afilla—*
sandpaper voice. Good Gitano voice: *Muy*	наждачный голос. Хороший голос гитано: *Muy*
rajo, very rough. Do you know	*rajo*, очень жесткий. А вы знаете

277

the worst thing
one can
say

about someone in
flamenco? No
me

dice nada. He
didn't say
anything

to me. He
didn't speak
something

I realized I
feared but
needed

to hear. Ay!
All these
stanzas

are rough! Or
worse, too
gentle.

They fumble. Earnest
as cows
and

they fumble. Do
you know
what

would be the
worst thing
said

что самое ужасное
что можно
сказать

о ком-то во
фламенко? No
me

dice nada. Он
ничего не
сказал

мне. Он не
произнес ничего
что

как выяснилось
было страшно
но

нужно услышать. Ау!
Все эти
строфы

так жестки! Или
хуже, слишком
мягки.

Они спотыкаются. Серьезные
как коровы
и

они спотыкаются. Знаете
ли вы
что

было бы мне
хуже всего
услышать

about my poetry?	о моих стихах?
I created	Не создала
nothing	ничего
that moved you.	что вас тронуло.
Made you	Заставило вас
cry	расплакаться
as if pain	как будто боль
was the	была одним
only	единственным
proof possible for	возможным доказательством
being alive.	того
So	что мы
	жили.
who among you	Так кто из
listening will	вас слушающих
be	будет
the wild dog	той дикой собакой
I am	которую я
calling?	зову?
Show me your	Покажите мне свой
snarl. Reveal	рык. Обнажите
your	свой
fangs. How can	клык. Как я
I sing	могу воспевать
blood	кровь
if I don't	если я не
bleed? Show	кровоточу? Покажите
me	мне
yourself as the	себя как тех
one for	за кого
whom	я

I will rip my own skin.	порву в клочья свою собственную кожу.
Show yourself before you bore me	Покажитесь прежде чем мне станет скучно
with your patient stalking. Show yourself	от вашей терпеливой слежки. Покажите как
darkened further by my orders. My	вы темнеете от моих приказов. Мои
people trained me. There is no	люди выучили меня. И нет никакого
shame in begging for what will	стыда в просьбах о том что
part my lips— what will trade	раскроет мои губы – о том что
caresses with my tongue—what will	обменяется ласками с моим языком – что
battle my teeth and make me	поборется с зубами и бросит в
sweat. My people trained me. I	пот. Мои люди выучили меня. Я

learned knives are sharp by being	узнала что ножи остры от своих
cut. I learned fires are hot	порезов. Я узнала что огонь горяч
by being burned. I learned to	от своих ожогов. Я выучилась топать
stamp my heels to sound like	пятками по земле со звуком похожим
a machine-gun blast because...*because...* Show	на автоматную очередь потому... *потому* ... Покажитесь –
yourself—I have a song to	у меня есть песня которой я
turn you into ice, then shatter!	превращу вас в лед и разобью!
Ole! Verdad! Show yourself—do you	Ole! Verdad! Покажитесь мне – вы что
think I'm begging for a crust	думаете я прошу у вас корочку
of bread already half-eaten by cockroaches?!	хлеба которую уже наполовину сгрызли тараканы?!

La Loca

*In the green
morning I
wanted*

*to be a
heart. A
heart.*

*And at evening's
end, I
wanted*

*to be my
voice. A
nightingale.
—LO(R)CA*

She fell in
love. Poor
Juana.

Fell in love
with the
most

handsome man in
the kingdom.
How

did the Prince
requite her
love?

By betraying her
with every
woman

La Loca

*Одним зеленым ранним
утром я
хотела*

*быть сердцем. Я
хотела быть
сердцем.*

*А в конце
вечера я
хотела*

*быть просто своим
голосом. Голосом
соловья.
—LO(R) CA*

Она взяла и
влюбилась. Бедная
Хуана.

Она взяла и
влюбилась в
самого

красивого мужчину во
всем королевстве.
Как

же принц ответил
на ее
любовь?

Он изменял ей
со всеми
женщинами

who simpered across his path. By	которые хихикнули на его пути. Он
lashing a florid sky across her	высек цветущий небосвод на ее
skin. By cutting her beautiful hair.	коже. Он остриг ее прекрасные волосы.
Poor Juana—always looking behind her	Бедная Хуана – вечно глядит назад через
stooped shoulders. How her Prince mocked	ссутуленные плечи. Как насмехался принц над
her, chilling her tears into multiple	ней, замораживая её слёзы в много
strands of pearls. Still, when he	разных ниток жемчуга. Но когда он
died, Juana went mad. She clawed	умер, Хуана утратила рассудок. Она драла
her cheeks and confused dogs into	ногтями щеки и сбитые с толку
whimpers, then howls. She rode throughout	обаки скулили, выли. Она проехала Всю

Granada keening over her Prince's coffin	Гранаду причитая над гробом своего принца
in a gloomy carriage pulled by	в мрачной карете с упряжкой из
eight horses. She rode and rode	восьми лошадей. Она ехала и ехала
with his stench becoming hers until	и его вонь становилась её пока
they both stunk up all of	они оба не завоняли на всю
Espana. She refused to bury him,	Эспанью. Она отказывалась хоронить его, умоляя
begging faces she concocted from receding	те лица что она лепила из
knotholes of trees passed by their	удаляющихся дупл деревьев несущихся мимо их
carriage, begging faces she drew by	кареты, умоляя лица нарисованные ею путем
connecting the stars pockmarking the irritated	соединения линиями звезд покрывавших сыпью раздраженное

night sky, begging faces she surfaced	ночное небо, умоляя лица которые всплывали
from bonfire smokes and crumpled balls	в дыму костров и смятых комьях
of sodden handkerchiefs. Her plea? She	мокрых носовых платков. О чём? Она
pleaded for his resurrection. Bah.	молила о его воскрешении. Ха.
She pleaded as if he would	Она молила как будто он мог
return to her if he came	вернуться к ней как будто мог
to breathe again. Bah. As if	снова начать дышать. Ха. Как будто
he once was there for her.	он когда-то был ей верной подмогой.
As if he ever wrote Poetry	Как будто он когда-то посвящал ей
for her. Now, do not misunderstand:	Стихи. Да, правда не нужно заблуждаться:

We gitanas adore
Juana The
"Crazy".

To honor her,
we cross
ourselves

and touch our
hair. We
honor

her because Juana
never faltered
from

living her Truth
even as
lies

snuffed the votive
lights in
her

eyes. Dame la
verdad. Poor
Juana.

   Once, I stepped
   into a
   story...

I love Juana.
But I
loathe

her, too. Once,
I courted
madness

мы, гитаны, обожаем
нашу «Безумную»
Хуану.

В честь её
мы крестимся
перстами

и трогаем свои
волосы. Мы
чтим

её потому что
Хуана твердо
стояла

на своей Правде
даже когда
ложь

гасила огоньки церковных
свечек в
ее

глазах. Dame la
verdad. Бедная
Хуана.

   Однажды, я попала
   в одну
   историю...

Я люблю Хуану.
Однако я
также

ненавижу ее. Однажды
я привлекла
безумие

for Poetry. But
I punched
through

that blur—grew
back my
hair.

Does it matter
that its
harvest

now elicits snow?
I punched
through

that silver, shimmery
blur. Ole!
I

grew back my
hair! So
what

if Winter has
become my
veil?

   I thought the
   story was
   mine...

I grew back
my hair.
I

love my refuge.
It veils
me

ради Поэзии. Но
я пробилась
свозь

то пятно – отрастила
себе волосы
снова.

Имеет ли значение
что их
урожай

теперь приносит снег?
Я пробилась
сквозь

то серебряное мерцающее
пятно. Ole!
Я

отрастила себе волосы
снова! И
что

что Зима теперь
стала моей
вуалью?

   Я думала что
   эта история
   моя...

Я снова отрастила
себе волосы.
Я

люблю свое пристанище.
Оно затуманивает
меня

into believing that when I write	и я верю что когда пишу
of Juana The Mad, I am	о своей Безумной Хуане, тогда я
still young with glossy, blue-black hair.	еще молода с блестящими, иссиня-черными волосами.
That when I write my poems	Что когда я пишу свои стихи
Juana is a subject and not	Хуана есть предмет стихов а не
the one releasing the wind that	то что выпускает тот ветер что
flares my skirts high to reveal	раздувает мои юбки выше чтобы обнажить
absolutely furious footwork —en compas— conjuring	абсолютно бешеную чечетку – en compas – вызывающую
up the ghosts of those who	к нам сюда духов тех кто
laugh at my red eyes— dark	насмехается над моими красными глазами – темных

angels who taught: there is no	ангелов которые учили что нет никакого
madness. There is only a woman	безумия. Что есть только одна женщина
brutishly in love. Hear me read	которая жестоко влюблена. Слушайте как я
me singing to You the A.	читаю вам и пою вам А.
The E. The I. The O.	Пою Э. Пою И. Пою О.
The U. The You. The U.	Пою Ы. Ты, Вы. Пою Ы.
And the Y. Hear me and	И пою У. Слышите, я пою
Juana dance! The seduction of flowers	а Хуана танцует! Соблазняются цветы прекрасные
blossoming into vowels. Hear me y	расцветают в гласные. Слышите, я и
Juana sing the machinegun blast of	Хуана поём эту автоматную очередь звуков

The A, The
I, The
E,

The O, The
U. Hear
us

die from the
Song of
Y,

the Dance of
Why? Listen
all

you nightingales! Why?
I curse
all

you nightingales! Why?
En compas/s!
I

thought it was
only a
story.

I thought the
story was
mine:

a bird caws
from my
mirror.

My mirror spits
out bloodied
feathers.

Поём А, поём
И, поём
Э,

Поём О, поём
У. Слушайте
Как

мы умираем от
Песни про
У,

от Танца про
Почему? Слушайте
все

вы соловьи! Почему?
Я проклинаю
всех

вас соловьев! Почему?
En compas/s!
Я

думала что это
была просто
история.

Я думала что
история была
моей:

как птица каркает
из моего
зеркала.

Мое зеркало выплевывает
покрытые кровью
перья.

I love you nightingales! All of	Я люблю вас соловьи! Каждого из
you! Why, dear nightingales? Why? Y	вас! Почему, милые соловьи? Почему? У
WHY? Y WHY?	ПОЧЕМУ? У ПОЧЕМУ?

As If	**Как будто**
There was *un* *momento*, a poem	Был один *un* *momento*, один стих
I wrote while driving the car.	который я написала за рулем машины.
My ego would not let me	Моё эго не могло позволить мне
pull over to jot it down.	остановиться у обочины чтобы записать его.
"If a poem is so powerful	«Если твое стихотворение и правда мощное
it will return," I have boasted	оно еще вернется», бывало, хвасталась я
for a long time to other	довольно долгое время в компании других

poets, as if
I possessed
some

knowledge they did
not already
know.

It feels like
years and
yet
that poem has
not yet
returned.

What I recall
is that,
somehow,

it related to
perfect timing
y

flamenco.

поэтов, как будто
я имела
некие

познания которых они
еще не
обрели.

Кажется, прошли годы
и годы
однако
то стихотворение так
и не
вернулось.

Но я помню
то что
как-то

оно связано с
безупречным ритмом
у

flamenco.

JULY

*"The 2018 wildfire season
was the deadliest and
most destructive wildfire
season in California"*
—Wikipedia

You walk out into ash
To discover the world's on fire

But we already knew that—

The Great Grief's Tankas

*This more-than-personal sadness
is what I call the "Great Grief "—a
feeling that rises in us as if from
the Earth itself.... that our
individual grief and emotional loss
can actually be a reaction to the
decline of our air, water, and
ecology* —Per Espen Stoknes
(Norwegian psychologist)

As plastic smothers
Oceans and forests miss trees
I grieve with you, Dear
We drink polluted water—
"Ethics of entanglement"

*

ИЮЛЬ

*«Сезон лесных пожаров 2018 г.
был самым разрушительным и
смертоносным сезоном
лесных пожаров в
Калифорнии».*
– Википедия

Вы выходите в пепел
Обнаруживаете что мир в огне

Но мы это и так уже знали –

Танка Великого Горя

*Ту печаль, что больше личной,
я называю Великим Горем –
чувством, которое как бы
поднимается прямо из самой
Земли... что наше
индивидуальное горе и
эмоциональные потери могут
на самом деле быть реакцией
на ухудшение воздуха, воды и
экологии* – Пер Эспен Стокнес,
норвежский психолог

Пластмасса душит
Океан и лес весь пуст
Вот горе, Милый
Мы пьем грязную воду –
«Этика причастности»

*

Drought in the desert
Cut through the cactus to see
Interior as dry
As the cracked sod surrounding
You, for whom no one sheds tears

*

When dinosaurs ruled
Skies rarely lapsed to yellows
King Midas' false gold
Within a blue, velvet box
Your pearls become small citrons

*

When the ocean grieves
Its anguish can't be discerned
Water swallows tears
I insist the faucet broke
Spraying my cheeks with non-tears

*

Where waterfalls end
Your face welcomes the cool spray
You admire beauty
From wet silver eroding
Mountains aware of their death

*

Storm season arrives
Snow falls beyond the window
Whitening the world
Yet its lack of sound cancels
Belief—as if worlds don't fall

*

Сухо в пустыне
Кактус разрежу смотри
Он сухой внутри
Как грунт в трещинах вокруг
Тебя, ненужного всем

*

При динозаврах
Небо редко желтело
Слюдой Мидаса
В синем бархате ларца
Твой жемчуг мелкий цитрон

*

Океан в горе
Его тоску не видно
Вода пьет слёзы
Поверьте сломался кран
Облил щеки не-слезой

*

Край водопада
Брызги радуют лицо
Ты восхищён красой
Жидкого серебра что
Точит смертные горы

*

Вот сезон штормов
Снег падает за окном
Обеляя мир
Его беззвучность глушит
Веру – будто мир стоит

*

Black cat against night
Against thoughts as the world
burns
Like children playing
Hide-and-seek in parks so bright
No one stumbled on omens

*

"Despair for the world"
Grew, leading him to water
Floating on the lake
He waits for peace, not knowing
Hunters shot the great heron

*

We'd grimly thinned trees
To prepare for winter's winds
But the leaves still fell
Tree limbs still broke. How did we
Come to trust preparation?

Черный кот в ночи
Фоном мысль а мир горит
Как дети в прятки
Играют в ярких парках
Не наступив на знаки

*

«Мировая скорбь»
Росла, привела к воде
По волне плывя
Он ждёт мира, не зная
Что цаплю застрелили

*

Лес проредили
Готовясь к зимним ветрам
Но листья пали
Сломались ветви. Что ж мы
Верили в подготовку?

Banog (Kite)

The Philippine Eagle is the Philippines' most evolutionarily distinct and globally endangered species.
—The Zoological Society of London

Under duress,
knowing forests are
reducing themselves into
ants, the eagles
insist on washing ashore
nude without feathers
elevating their wings

Once upon a time
the Philippine Eagle
scoffed at Icarus—
the line between myth
and the 21st century
was tethered to earth
before it evaporated—

the line between myth
and the 21st century
is humanity's profile

Banog (Змей)

Филиппинский орел – самый эволюционно особенный вид под самой большой глобальной угрозой исчезновения. – Лондонское зоологическое общество

Под принуждением,
зная, что леса
сокращают себя до
муравьев, орлы
упорно выбрасываются на берег
голые без перьев
возвышая крылья

Давным-давно
Филиппинский Орел
высмеивал Икара –
граница между мифом
и 21-м веком
была привязана к земле
пока не испарилась –

граница между мифом
и 21-м веком
есть профиль человечества

The Return of DoveLion

7: I forgot there is a country somewhere on the opposite of where I stand on this earth, a country whose scents stubbornly perfume my dreams.

47: I forgot mud in monsoon season always sucked at the ankles, non-discriminating, a placid surface but camouflaging sharply edged stones, gooooey, gooooey, gooooey and brown as the hide on rotten bananas.

93: I forgot appreciating a *delicadeza* moonlight as much as any long-haired maiden.

50: I forgot farmers who never lost their smiles as their skins grew permanently stained from water buffalo excrement spread over surrounding fields during days of absent storms.

65: I forgot elders who always grinned at me, unashamed their gums held no teeth.

Возвращение ГолубеЛьва

7: Я забыла, что где-то напротив того места, на котором я стою на этой земле, есть страна, чьи запахи упрямо летают в моих снах.

47: Я забыла что грязь муссонного сезона всегда засасывает лодыжки, без разницы, гладкая поверхность но она прячет остроугольные камни лиипкая, лиипкая, лиипкая и бурая как шкуры гнилых бананов.

93: Я забыла как ценила *delicadeza* луну как любая другая длинноволосая дева.

50: Я забыла фермеров которые не теряли улыбок в то время как их кожу навсегда окрашивали экскременты водяных буйволов разбросанные по окрестным полям в дни без штормов.

65: Я забыла старейшин которые всегда улыбались мне, не стыдясь своих беззубых десен.

3: I forgot the light burned and we never shaded our eyes.

46: I forgot discovering the limited utility of calm seas.

78: I forgot children learning to trick hunger with cups of weak tea.

80: I forgot fevers refusing to abate even when drenched with salty waves.

82: I forgot narrowing the focus always reveals something else.

51: I forgot lowering the flag of a country I despised. I forgot lowering the flag of a country I loved.

12: I forgot the stance of cliffs meeting water.

97: I forgot I began drowning in air.

101: I forgot you were the altar that made me stay.

3: Я забыла что свет был ярким и мы никогда не берегли от него глаз.

46: Я забыла как открыла ограниченную полезность спокойного моря.

78: Я забыла как дети учатся обманывать голод при помощи чашки слабого чая.

80: Я забыла как лихорадка отказывается униматься даже при погружении в соленые волны.

82: Я забыла что суженный фокус всегда обнажает что-то новое.

51: Я забыла как спускали флаг страны которую я ненавидела. Я забыла как спускали флаг страны которую я любила.

12: Я забыла как стоят скалы при встрече с водой.

97: Я забыла как начала тонуть в воздухе.

101: Я забыла что ты был алтарем заставившим меня остаться.

99: I forgot the spine bent willingly for a stranger's whip.

100: I forgot clutching the wet mane of a panicked horse.

101: I forgot night is unanimous.

102: I forgot how an erasure captures the threshold of consciousness.

103: I forgot how one begins marking time from a lover's utterance of *Farewell*.

110: I forgot learning to appreciate rust, and how it taught me bats operate through radar.

113: I forgot admiring women who refuse to paint their lips.

114: I forgot dust motes trapped in a tango after the sun lashed out a ray.

120: I forgot the colors of a scream: the regret of crimson, the futility of pink, the astonishment of brown.

122: I forgot your favorite color was water.

99: Я забыла про позвоночник послушно согнутый под плетью иноземца.

100: Я забыла как хваталась за мокрую гриву испуганной лошади.

101: Я забыла что ночь единогласна.

102: Я забыла как стирание ловит порог сознания.

103: Я забыла как начинают отсчет времени со слова любовника *Прощай.*

110: Я забыла как научилась ценить ржавчину, и как она открыла мне что летучие мыши летают по радару.

113: Я забыла как восхищалась женщинами которые отказываются красить губы.

114: Я забыла охваченные танго пылинки в луче выброшенном солнцем.

120: Я забыла цвета крика: сожаление алого, напрасность розового, остолбенение коричневого.

122: Я забыла что вода твой любимый цвет.

123: I forgot admiring Picasso's *Sleeping Nude, 1907*, for its lack of sentimentality.

123: Я забыла как меня восхитила «Спящая обнаженная» Пикассо (1907) своим отсутствием сентиментальности.

124: I forgot aching for fiction that would not chasten my days.

124: Я забыла как нуждалась в прозе не карающей мои дни.

128: I forgot becoming my own sculpture when I crawled on a floor to see color from different angles.

128: Я забыла как стала скульптурой себя ползая по полу чтобы разглядеть цвет с разных углов.

129: I forgot astonishment over a block of grey metal swallowing light.

129. Я забыла ошеломительный эффект блока серого металла поглощающего свет.

72: I forgot feeling you in the air against my cheek.

72. Я забыла как почувствовала тебя в воздухе овевавшем мне щеку.